THE WEAVER'S TALE

THE WEAVER'S TALE

Kate Sedley

St. Martin's Press
New York

THE WEAVER'S TALE. Copyright © 1993 by Kate Sedley. All rights reserved. Printed in the United States of America. No part of this book may be used or reproduced in any manner whatsoever without written permission except in the case of brief quotations embodied in critical articles or reviews. For information, address St. Martin's Press, 175 Fifth Avenue, New York, N.Y. 10010.

Library of Congress Cataloging-in-Publication Data

Sedley, Kate.
The weaver's tale / Kate Sedley.
p.   cm.
ISBN 0-312-10474-X (hardcover)
1. Roger the Chapman (Fictitious character)—Fiction.
2. Great Britain—History—Wars of the Roses, 1455–1485—
Fiction.   3. Peddlers and peddling—England—Fiction.
I. Title.
PR6069.E323W4   1994
823'.914—dc20   93-44039   CIP

First published in Great Britain by HEADLINE BOOK PUBLISHING LTD.

First U.S. Edition: April 1994
10   9   8   7   6   5   4   3   2   1

THE WEAVER'S TALE

Chapter One

It was a cold winter's day when I first met Lillis and her mother, Margaret Walker. Christmas of 1473 had come and gone. The Lord of Misrule had put aside his cap and bells for another year and the Boy Bishops had doffed their borrowed mitres. Although already January, traces of the previous month's snow were still to be found in sheltered places. The Earl of Oxford continued to be holed up on St Michael's Mount, slowly being starved into submission by the Cornish sheriff and his men and the vigilant captains of the royal fleet. Whenever and wherever possible, people stayed warm and snug within doors to avoid the icy winds and the stinging rain which had made life miserable for the past few days.

As I wove my unsteady course along the deserted market-place, the great bulk of Bristol castle towered ahead of me, the donjon rearing its ugly face to peer malevolently across the intervening inner ward, which in its turn was rimmed by high, grim walls. My pack weighed with unaccustomed heaviness on my back, and my legs felt as though they were made of lead. In contrast, my head was so light it might have been stuffed with feathers, like the goose-feather mattress my mother had owned and been so proud of. My forehead burned to the touch, yet my hands and feet were cold as stone.

I think it would be no idle boast to say that I have enjoyed almost unfailing good health throughout my life, at least until recent years. I have always been strong and able, but that means that on those rare occasions when illness strikes, it lays me extremely low. The ague which had me in its grip that day had taken hold a sennight earlier. I had been making my way westward after a profitable autumn and early winter peddling my wares among the villagers and hamlet-dwellers around Southampton. The pleasant sun-dappled days of late October had given way to an unusually warm November, engendering a feeling of contentment and well-being. This was augmented by the recollection of my recent trip to Brittany, and the satisfaction of knowing that I had successfully discharged the obligations thrust upon me by the Duke of Gloucester. But that's another story. Suffice it to say that the sudden fall of snow and icy rains which struck that Christmas in the south, found me ill-prepared to withstand their violent blast. Within a week of Our Saviour's birthday, I awoke one morning in the outlying barn of a manor somewhere north of Salisbury, to find myself shaking and sweating with a fever, and my night's companion bending over me, his face puckered with concern. He was a Carmelite friar who, caught by the previous evening's

storm, had been deterred from seeking better accommodation, and who had shared both my humble shelter
and my supper. Fortunately my appetite had been small,
a circumstance which in itself should have warned me
that all was not well.

'You're ill, my son,' he had said, feeling my brow with
a calloused hand.

'Nonsense!' I retorted. 'I'm never ill. This seizure will
pass. I must be on my way as soon as I have broken
my fast.'

He regarded me dubiously, crouched on his haunches
at my feet, his white habit mud-splattered to the knees by
filth from the roads, wisps of hay from his makeshift bed
still stuck in his hair.

'I doubt you're fit enough to travel but, if you must,
then make for your winter quarters as soon as maybe.'

With a great effort, I controlled my trembling limbs. 'I
have no winter quarters.'

The bushy eyebrows came together in a frown. 'You
mean you travel the roads in all seasons?' When I nodded,
he threw up his hands in astonishment. 'But that's madness! I've never met a traveller of any sort who did not
have some base for winter months. A snug billet with
wife or mother or leman where he can lie up during the
cold and wet and live on the summer's profits. And in
your line of business, you can always take advantage of
more clement days to sally forth into the surrounding
countryside and make a little extra money by selling your
goods among neighbouring communities.' He patted my

arm in avuncular fashion. 'Heed my advice, my son, and go home to your mother.'

'She's dead,' I answered shortly.

'You must have other kin who will house you during the winter.'

I shook my head, but stopped abruptly when I found it made my senses reel. 'There's no one.'

The friar was not to be so easily defeated. 'Friends?' he suggested. 'Your parish priest? Tell me where you were born, lad.'

'Wells. My father was a stone-carver in the cathedral.'

'Then surely you must have some acquaintances in the city. Can you think of no one who would be willing to offer you lodgings in return for payment?' He added, sinking his voice to a lower level, 'The best thing you can do, my son, is marry. Find yourself a good woman who will make a home for you to go back to every winter, and who will maintain it while you are away each summer.' He dug me slyly in my aching ribs. 'It seems to me the perfect life, much to be envied, and I wonder you have not thought of it for yourself. The comfort of your own hearth on the one hand and the freedom of being your own man on the other. A wife to cosset and fuss over you when the wind and rain rattle the shutters, but all the world your oyster when sun and gentle breezes make you restless and fancy-free.'

Only half of what he said penetrated my befuddled senses at the time, although I was later to find that I could recall all of this unclerical advice almost word for word.

But the idea that I should make for home did stick in my mind long after the friar had taken his leave and gone; an idea which suddenly seemed eminently desirable. He was right: there must still be people who remembered me in Wells and who had borne a kindness towards my mother. And some goodwife would be thankful for a little extra money until better weather once again made living easier in the spring.

From where I was, Wells lay in a north-westerly direction, along well-trodden paths and tracks across country, at least twenty miles south of Bristol. How I came to go so far astray could be attributed to the fall of snow, which had obliterated so many familiar landmarks, and to my feverish condition which steadily worsened with each passing day. Both plausible reasons and few sensible men would dispute them. But I am not so sure. I suspect that God had taken a hand and was bending me to His Will, forcing me yet again to be the instrument of His Divine Purpose; using my talent for unravelling mysteries to prevent villainy from going undetected. Why else should I have fallen sick at that particular moment? Why should the friar have suggested I go home? And why should I have missed my way, ending up a score or so miles further north, in Bristol? If my children ever read this they will smile indulgently, pitying an old man's fancies; and indeed I am half inclined to mock myself. But the suspicion lingers; and a lifetime of fighting and arguing and trying to outwit God, all to no avail, only increases my conviction. For the fact remains that some nine months

5

after Robert Herepath was hanged for a murder he did not commit, I staggered into Bristol and straight into the very heart of a mystery.

I turned right, making my way beneath the shelter of the castle walls, over the bridge spanning the Frome, past the weir and castle mill and along the banks of the river in the direction of the Pithay Gate. Through thick drizzle, I could just see the outlines of the Dominican friary which stands in the broad meadows beyond the city. The afternoon was drawing to a close and darkness already encroaching. Someone had lit cressets on one of the friary outbuildings to guide travellers on their way and ensure that they did not miss their footing, ending up in the muddy waters of the Frome. The gatekeeper at the Pithay Bridge was cold and growing churlish. He plainly wanted to lock up for the night, and return to his family and the warmth of his house, but it lacked some time to curfew.

He nodded brusquely, and had started to demand my business in the city, when he paused, peering more closely at me. 'You look ill, my lad.' His gaze sharpened with suspicion. 'Anything serious?'

I sneezed violently and shook my head. 'A rheum, that's all, through sleeping in the open.'

'At this time of year?' His voice echoed the disbelief of the friar.

'I'm a pedlar,' I snapped. 'I peddle my wares around the countryside.'

'There's no need for that tone!' he retorted. 'Most trav-

---

ellers I've ever met go to ground in winter, if they've any sense.' He subjected me to further scrutiny, finally deciding that I was suffering from nothing more serious than I had claimed. He jerked his head at the opposite archway. 'You can pass. But I'd find a good soft bed for the night if I were you. You look as though you need it.'

I nodded briefly and made my way into the castle foregate. To my left, I could see St Peter's Church and Hospital, but instead of making for its sheltering warmth, I lurched towards the city cross where Wine Street met High Street, Broad Street and Corn Street. I remembered that the New Inn stood close to All Hallows Church and, failing that, there was the Full Moon serving St James's Priory. I kept my eyes fixed on the tower of St Ewen's, the parish church of the wealthy residential quarter of the town, which is frequented by many of the rich merchants and burgesses. Bristol then was nearly as prosperous as it is today, although now the voyages of the Cabots have poured yet more money into its coffers. Its walls house a closely knit community, whose face is necessarily turned away from Europe towards Ireland, and it has many links of trade and blood with that turbulent island.

It was almost dark. The drizzle was turning to mist, covering men's clothes and beards with drops of moisture. Shops were being shuttered for the night, their owners retiring to the living quarters at the back or, if they were stalls, being locked and barred while the proprietors hurried away across the cobbles to more modest, but no less inviting, accommodation elsewhere in the city. The

High Cross loomed in front of me and I hesitated, as much to get my breath as from indecision. I was shaking from head to foot, and a cold sweat had broken out all over my body. A torch flared with a noise like torn parchment, high on a house wall somewhere to my left. By its wavering light, I was dimly aware of two women making their way up High Street, but whether they were old or young or both, I could not have said at that juncture. I was only conscious of an overwhelming desire to lie down where I was and close my eyes on an increasingly hostile landscape which refused to stand still, shifting and swaying whenever I tried to focus my eyes. I reached out for the support of the cross and leaned my forehead against its cold stone.

A hand touched my shoulder and a high, clear, slightly childish voice called, 'Mother! Over here! I think this young man is sick.'

Wooden pattens clattered across the cobbles and a maturer voice asked, 'What's the matter, Lillis? What are you saying? It will be dark soon and we haven't any time to waste.' Then there was an exclamation of concern and dismay. Another hand, larger than the first, gripped my shoulder. 'What is it, lad? Are you ill?'

I nodded, unable to speak. I could feel my knees begin to buckle and I held on desperately to my column of the High Cross in an effort to remain upright.

The second voice continued, 'Where do you live?' But the first woman, address as Lillis, must have noticed my pack.

'He's a chapman, Mother. He's probably just passing through.'

I nodded my head, foolishly opening my eyes as I did so. The world somersaulted and I was promptly sick, heaving up what little food I had eaten in the past few hours on the roadway. With a sigh, I subsided in an ungainly heap.

The older woman was giving instructions to her daughter and, at the same time, shooing back the little crowd of onlookers which had gathered to find out what was going on. Any diversion was welcome on a miserable late afternoon in winter.

'Run back across the bridge, Lillis, and fetch some of the men to help carry him home. He can't be left like this, poor lad. He's in a fever. You and I must care for him until he's better. And what are you lot gawping at? Stand clear and give him room. How can he breathe with you fools bending over him?' There was an uneasy muttering in which I caught the word 'plague'. My benefactress gave a snort of derision. 'At this time of year? There's nothing wrong with him but a rheum which has become feverish with neglect and too much sleeping rough. I've met big, strong lads like this one before. They all think themselves Samsons and take no heed of their bodies' needs until those same bodies rebel. With good nursing he'll be as good as new in a couple of weeks.'

Their worst fears allayed, most of the onlookers seemed to disperse. I dared not open my eyes again to check, but I heard the shuffle of their departure and felt, rather than saw, the open space around me. But someone must have remained, for a man's gruff tones objected, 'You want to take heed of yourself, Margaret Walker, two women living alone as you and Lillis do, before taking a strange man into your home. A chapman! He could cut your throats and be off with your purse one of these nights, while you're both sleeping.'

'If we're dead, we won't be sleeping, you silly old man!' was the acid retort. 'Don't you think I've lived long enough in this world, Nick Brimble, to know an honest face when I see one?'

There was a grunt which could have indicated either agreement or scepticism: I had no means of telling with my eyes fast shut. But after a moment, the man called Brimble warned, 'I'm only thinking of you and Lillis. You've had more than your fair share of misfortune these past ten months.'

Margaret Walker, taking no thought for the dirt on the cobbles, had knelt down beside me and was gently pillowing my head on her breast, supporting my sagging body with her slender frame. From her voice, I had imagined her – insofar as I was capable of imagining anything at that moment – as a woman of ample proportions, and I was vaguely surprised at the narrowness of her bony shoulder.

Her head, which she had bent towards me, reared indignantly at the man's words. 'These last ten months! You have a short memory, Nick Brimble! And me a widow for seventeen years come May! A good man and a young son lost in an accident that should never have happened!'

'The will of God,' Nick Brimble murmured piously.

'The fault of a drunken carter who was too sodden with drink to control his horse properly when the beast took fright and bolted!' Her voice was bitter with suppressed rage.

'The will of God all the same,' her friend stoutly maintained. 'But this last misfortune . . .' There was a pause and a sigh before he continued sombrely, 'The Devil had a hand in that, whatever the truth of it, and I doubt if we'll ever know that now. Your father was the only one who could have unravelled the mystery, and he's taken his secret to the grave.'

Before the woman had time to answer, there was a call of 'Mother!' and once again the clatter of pattens on cobbles. A sudden flurry of skirts told me that the girl Lillis had returned and, judging by the deeper male tones in her wake, had brought the required assistance with her. 'How is he?'

'He'll do, but he'll be all the better for getting to bed with a hot brick at his feet and some decent blankets over him. 'You've brought a litter. Good. Nick, if you've nothing more important to do, lend Hob and Burl a hand to get the lad hoisted. He'll be a decent weight, I reckon. Burl, you take his legs and Hob and Nick his head. That's right. That's got him.'

I felt myself lifted bodily and placed on the blanket slung between two poles, which had been laid near me on the ground. I ventured a quick upward glance between my lashes, but it was now almost completely dark, in addition to which that single effort had once more started me retching. My pack had been removed from my shoulders, and Lillis was instructed by her mother to bring it with her and to stop grumbling because it was heavy.

'You may deceive others with that fragile look of yours, my girl, but you don't fool me. You're as strong and wiry as a mule.'

Her daughter muttered rebelliously beneath her breath, but struggled obediently with the pack, which fortunately was none too full just at that present. As for me, I was too far gone to suffer any pangs of conscience. I had been rescued by two Good Samaritans, and that was all I knew or cared about. As we all set off down High Street, Hob and Burl each carrying one end of the litter, my long-suffering body jolted roughly from side to side as they made for 'home', wherever that was, I thankfully let my worries slide and gave myself up to the prospect of a warm bed and the ministrations of a pair of capable women. As we plunged into the dark canyon of Bristol Bridge, the houses and shops rearing up on either hand, I was once again violently sick before mercifully losing consciousness.

Chapter Two

During the next few days, I lay in that twilight state, half waking, half sleeping, between sanity and nightmare, when evil seems to gibber at the edges of the senses and has to be fought with might and main to be held at bay. Only on three occasions before the fever finally abated did I have moments of conscious clarity.

The first time, I think, must have been briefly on the morning following my arrival, for just long enough to remember what had happened and to take in my surroundings. I had been undressed and was wearing a clean linen shift a size or so too small for me. The material was strained across my chest and had already split a little near the top of one of the sleeves. I was lying on a straw-filled mattress, covered with a couple of rough blankets which smelled sweetly of dried lavender, close to a central hearth. A fire of driftwood and sea coal, both doubtless scavenged for along the shores of the tidal River Avon, belched smoke through a hole in the roof of the cottage's single room. An adjustable pot-hook hung from the metal crossbar of a cooking crane, and from the hook was suspended a sizeable iron pot which made bubbling noises as well as giving forth the smell of a good broth; an aroma which at any other time would have made my mouth water, but then only made me heave.

I closed my eyes for a moment and did not open them again until my stomach had settled. This second glance informed me that a spinning-wheel stood near the only window whose shutters were open, allowing the pallid daylight of a January day to filter through the oiled-parchment pane. The dim outline of a bed, large enough to a accommodate two people, could be seen at one end of the room, while a chest, a table, two stools, a wooden bench and a narrow cupboard were ranged around the walls. Recollecting the direction in which I had been carried in the litter, down the gentle slope of High Street and across Bristol Bridge, my previous experience of the city, nearly three years old now but still vividly remembered, told me that I was in the Redcliffe district where the weavers had their quarters, huddled in the lee of St Thomas's Church. There were rich dwellings here, as I recalled, but this was a weaver's cottage. Or had been, I guessed, when Mistress Walker's husband was alive; and it said much for the master that he had not turned her and her daughter out after the man's untimely death, although she was undoubtedly valuable as a spinner.

That was my last thought as I drifted once more into a semi-conscious state. The soft, low tones of women's voices, the rustle of their feet among the floor rushes, were only dimly heard; their gentle touch, as they washed and fed me and attended to more intimate needs, only vaguely felt. I had retreated again into darkness and a world where I either burned or froze, but which was never free of demons.

The second time I came to myself, it was night. Rush-lights burned in candle-holders set on table and chest. Shadows flickered and curtseyed across the walls. Margaret Walker was spinning by the light of a dying fire, while the girl Lillis sat and watched her. I realized with a shock that I had been moved to the comfort of the bed, and that the mattress I had lain on formerly was rolled up, together with the blankets, against one wall, and was, presumably, being used by the women. Had I been so ill that such a sacrifice was necessary? It must have been so, and indeed, when I made an attempt to move and call out, my limbs and voice refused to obey me. The most I could achieve was a feeble motion of one hand and a kind of strangled croak.

It was enough, however, to attract Lillis's attention and to bring her immediately to my side. 'He's awake, Mother,' she said, and the chatter of the spinning-wheel ceased.

Margaret Walker crossed the room in her deliberate, unhurried fashion, and smiled down at me. 'Don't try to speak,' she instructed, placing a soothing hand on my forehead. 'I expect you're thirsty. Lillis, fetch water and put some of that dried lettuce-juice powder in it. It'll make him sleep and that's what he needs just now. You've been very sick,' she added, confirming my own suspicions, 'and it will take a day or so yet before you're fit enough to be allowed out of bed.' She took the beaker handed to her by Lillis and held it to my lips. 'Get this down. It will do you good.' She propped up my shoulders while I drank, then lowered me back on to the pillows. 'Can you manage to tell me your name?' she asked. 'It's difficult not knowing what to call you.'

'Roger,' I whispered and closed my eyes. It worried me that I felt so weak, and that so little effort left me exhausted. I needed to get back on the road as soon as possible and to stop imposing on the charity of these good women.

Margaret seemed to read my thoughts. 'You're not to worry,' she admonished me. 'You must stay here until you are completely well. It's no hardship to us. In fact, it's a pleasure to me to have a man to look after again. I've missed the sense of purpose since my father died . . .' She broke off short, as though she had said more than she intended, and got up from her seat on the edge of the bed. 'There! Try to sleep now.'

She returned to her spinning-wheel, calling sharply to Lillis, who showed a tendency to linger at the bedside, smoothing my forehead with small, cold fingers. I smiled at the girl and let my eyelids droop, but continued watching her from beneath my lashes.

Lillis Walker was slight and very dark. Thin and plain, her huge brown eyes and coils of thick black hair were her two redeeming features. Her skin was sallow, her face elfin, and her body had the sharp angularity of a child's.

I still remember the surprise I felt when I learned that she was less than two years younger than myself, and was approaching her twentieth birthday. Her movements were quick and birdlike as she darted impulsively from one thing to another, her bright, inquiring gaze taking in everything around her. She had a strong Celtic strain, derived from her maternal grandmother, a Cornishwoman, and her father's people, who had originally come from Wales. All this, however, I learned much later, when I was up and about. That evening, as I lay and watched her as she returned reluctantly to her mother's side, I simply thought her a rather odd child.

The dried lettuce juice was starting to work its potent spell, lulling me once more into a troubled sleep, when there was a knock on the door which jerked me awake. Both women stared silently for a moment, first at the door, then at each other.

'Don't answer,' breathed Lillis.

The tapping came again, soft but persistent. With a resigned sigh, Margaret rose to her feet and drew back the bolts and bar before opening the door a crack. From where I was lying, the aperture was just wide enough to let me make out a shadowy form and the gleam of a lantern, partially obscured by a drape of black cloth. Whoever stood outside was evidently at pains not to advertise his presence as he went about his business through the dark streets. This reticence might simply have been the result of its being after curfew, but somehow I did not think so. Obedience to the bell was no longer as strictly enforced as it had been once upon a time, any more than curfew's original purpose of damping down fires was nowadays regularly observed.

I caught a low, indistinguishable murmur, then Margaret's voice sounding firm and clear. 'No. I've already told you, I don't want you here. I made my message plain after my father died. You waste your time and mine. Please go.'

The caller, however, was not so easily put off. Further mutterings followed until his unwilling listener lost her patience. 'No! And again, no! You and your kind have no place in this house any longer. Remove your foot or I shall send my girl for the Watch.' Margaret glanced over her shoulder. 'Lillis!'

But there was no need for Lillis to risk the night streets, as her mother had probably guessed. The threat of authority was sufficient to frighten her unwelcome visitor and make him withdraw in a hurry. There was something which sounded like a curse, the lantern bobbed and dipped and then the light disappeared. Margaret Walker shut and barred the door for the second time that evening, and returned to her seat by the fire. I expected her to be upset, but when she spoke, she sounded more angry than perturbed.

'I think they've realized I'm in earnest and won't bother us again. At least, let's hope so. If they do, then they'll have to understand . . .'

But what the mysterious 'they' would be made aware of, I was not at that point destined to know. The lettuce powder had done its work and I heard no more. I fell asleep as abruptly as a candle-flame is doused by the snuffers.

I have said that I had three moments of clarity during those early days of my illness, and of the two I have recounted, I was perfectly certain. They remained fixed in my memory long after I was up and about and taking my first cautious steps about the room. Of the third, however, I retained doubts for some time, until Lillis herself unblushingly assured me that it was true; that I had not dreamt it; that she had indeed crept naked into my bed to warm me when I was in the throes of one of the terrible shivering fits which seized me during the onset of the fever.

'You were so cold,' she said, propping her elbow on the table and cupping her chin in one hand. She regarded me unblinkingly across the narrow board, her gaze wide and limpid as though what she was admitting to was the most natural thing in the world. And so I might have thought it in this strange elfin creature, half woman, half child, except for a gleam of prurience lurking at the back of the eyes; those enormous dark eyes which seemed at times to be the whole of her face.

I could feel the hot colour mounting my cheeks, and was thankful that I had not yet found the energy to shave. A week's growth of strong, springy, blond hair was sufficient to mask my blushes.

My companion went on a little breathlessly. 'I only

asked if you remembered because you haven't mentioned what happened, and I wasn't sure if you did. Remember, I mean. And *if* you did, you might blurt it out in front of Mother, and she . . . well, she might not understand.'

This I could believe. I cleared my throat and answered as steadily as I was able, 'Yes, I do recall . . . That is, I thought what happened, happened. But I wasn't sure if I had dreamt it or not.'

Lillis gave her small, secretive smile and flicked me an upwards glance from beneath her long lashes. 'Oh no, you didn't dream it. It was that first night after we brought you home. You were on the mattress on the floor and Mother and I were in bed. She was fast asleep and so were you, but then in the early hours of the morning you grew restless, moaning and tossing. Then you began to shiver violently. Your teeth were chattering and you couldn't seem to get warm. I slid out of bed to put another piece of turf on the fire, but then . . . well . . . I thought it a better idea to get under the blankets with you and wrap you in my arms.' The smile deepened and the eyes became like a cat's: two gleaming slits. 'And it soothed you. After a while, you stopped shaking and fell asleep. So I stayed with you until the first crack of light showed through the shutters, when I crept back to bed. And not a moment too soon. Mother was stirring within minutes, but she suspected nothing, and there's no need that she should ever know.'

'I certainly shan't tell her,' I assured Lillis fervently.

She gave a little crow of laughter. 'You're embarrassed!

A great lad like you who's probably had a score of girls!
I wonder why.'

I would have been hard put to it myself to explain
why the thought of her naked body curled close to mine,
even though I knew nothing of it, made me so uncomfortable. She was right; there had been women in plenty these
past two years since, an innocent escaping from the
religious life, I had laid my first girl on the banks of
the River Stour, in far-off Kent. Was it because I already
suspected that she had marked me down as her own? The
huntress and her quarry.

It was late afternoon, some fortnight after I had entered
Bristol through the Pithay Gate, and for the fourth or fifth
day running I had been allowed to get up, wash and dress
myself and take a few tentative steps up and down the
room. Tomorrow I would definitely be rid of my beard,
and as soon as possible after that I must start looking for
other lodgings where I could stay until I was fit enough
to take to the road once more with my pack. I had insisted
on sleeping on the floor again at nights, thus enabling the
women to return to their bed, but the confined space was
becoming an embarrassment, as well as making me feel
hemmed in.

Margaret Walker, who had finished spinning for the
day, had taken her yarn to the weaving sheds, and would
be back presently with her two willow panniers dangling
from their shoulder-yoke and packed with new wool. Outside, the weather continued icy-cold and wet, the relent-
less spears of rain soaking the cobbles, making the stones

treacherous to walk on and causing the pack-animals to slither miserably beneath their loads. So much I had been able to observe from the open doorway before Lillis had scolded me back to the warmth of the fire. And it was when I had settled myself on a stool at one end of the table, my feet extended towards the blaze on the hearth, that she had come to sit opposite me and asked if I remembered her getting in beside me that first night.

Now, our conversation had petered out, and we sat in silence, Lillis continuing to watch me, more than ever like a cat with a mouse, while I resolutely avoided her gaze, staring into the burning heart of the fire. And it was thus that Margaret Walker found us when she at last returned, a gust of bitter wind almost lifting her off her feet as she came through the doorway, in spite of the heavy baskets hanging at her sides.

'You're both very quiet,' she said, lowering her burdens to the floor and unhooking them from the wooden yoke. She shook the drops of water from her cloak and put back her hood, exclaiming sharply as she did so, 'Lillis! Why haven't you begun to get the meal? You haven't even put the water on to boil, let alone prepared the vegetables for the pot.'

Lillis grimaced but, to her credit, she never took exception, however harsh her mother's tone, and sometimes Margaret's admonitions were unmerited. She rose good-humouredly to her feet, reached down the iron pot from its place on the shelf beside the door, and filled it from the water barrel in one corner. When I would have helped her carry it to the fire, Margaret told me shortly to sit down.

'You're not fit to lift things yet, and besides, we have to manage by ourselves when you're not here. We're both strong and able.'

I had to admit that Lillis, for all her apparent fragility, had great strength in her stick-like arms, and made no more ado about hooking the full pot on to the crossbar of the cooking crane than she might have done about lifting a jar of flowers. I retired once more to my stool, where I sat watching the two women chop up the herbs and root vegetables which provided the staple ingredients of the afternoon meal. For dinner, we had had some salted mutton with our broth, but a lump of bacon fat was considered sufficient to give whatever flavour was needed to our supper stew. And, ladled over a slice of wheat and rye bread, it would suffice to curb my swiftly reviving appetite.

Margaret looked up from her chopping and gave me a smile. 'You're beginning to get the colour back in your cheeks at last, what I can see of them under that beard.'

'It's coming off tomorrow,' I promised. I shifted uneasily on my stool, rightly foreseeing that my next words might cause trouble. 'And then I must be off, to Wells, if I can make it,' I added, coming to a sudden decision. 'It was where I was heading when I lost my way, coming up from Salisbury. It's my birthplace. I was hoping to renew some old acquaintance of my mother's and find a berth for the winter.'

The consternation on both their faces was writ large.

'But you can't think of walking twenty miles or more in your condition,' Margaret protested angrily. 'I've never heard such foolishness!'

'You have a place to stay. Here!' Lillis wailed. 'You can't desert us, not after all we've done for you!'

But this remark only diverted her mother's wrath on to Lillis's own head. 'What we've done, we've done because it was our Christian duty, my girl, and don't you forget it! It's not a weapon to force Roger's hand and make him do something he doesn't wish to.' Margaret turned back to me. 'Take no notice of her, lad. Never consider yourself beholden to us for a minute. I'm only thinking of your health, although I don't deny we'd both be glad of your company if you changed your mind and decided to stay. It's lonely, just the two of us, these long, dark nights.'

Lillis nodded agreement. 'Especially since Grandfather died and there's been all the whispering behind our backs. And sometimes people pass remarks openly within our hearing. As though what happened was our fault, or had anything to do with us! We're just as ignorant of the truth as the rest of them.' She caught Margaret's eye and added impatiently: 'He's going to hear the story sooner or later, Mother, if he stops, so he might as well hear it from us and not just anyone. At least what we tell him will be fact and not just rumour.' She laughed triumphantly. 'Look! I've aroused his interest, you can see it in his face. Who knows,' Lillis went on mockingly, 'Roger might even be able to resolve the mystery for us!'

Chapter Three

At Lillis's last words, I felt again that mounting sense of excitement blended with resentment which I had experienced twice before, on the two previous occasions when I had been sure that God was using me as His instrument of retribution. When I had discarded the religious life, some three years earlier and against my dead mother's wishes, to gain my independence on the open road, it had not occurred to me that God might demand some return for the loss of my poor services. But He had given me a cool-thinking brain and a sharp eye for detail which, allied with a tender conscience, had twice now caused me to turn aside from my own affairs and resolve those of others. And here I was, once more the recipient of an obvious cry for help by two women who had made me their debtor. For although Margaret Walker immediately distanced herself from her daughter's suggestions, her need for a sympathetic listener with whom to share whatever trouble she had was plain for me to see.

In a last, desperate bid for freedom, I said, 'It isn't fit

that two women should be sharing their cottage with a strange man, a single room housing the three of us. You'll find yourselves the subject of gossip, and I should be loath to have that laid at my door.'

Margaret paused in her vegetable chopping and glanced up with a derisive smile. 'Lad, I'm old enough to be your mother and, furthermore, I'm a respectable widow. So why should I not have the benefit of your intention to take permanent lodgings for the winter, rather than some woman in Wells? Surely I'm as deserving of your money as she is? And, as you know, there is an outside privy, and a curtain which we can pull to divide the room in two when privacy is needed indoors. As soon as you are fit again, you can as easily ply your trade around Bristol as Wells, and more than likely the pickings will be better. However, if you're determined to go, I can't stop you, but only wish you Godspeed.'

Her arguments were irrefutable, and my heart sank while she made them, for there was no escaping the fact that I owed her and Lillis more than I could adequately repay. At the same time, I felt that quickening of interest which Lillis's words had aroused, and could almost see the end of my nose quivering with anticipation, like a dog scenting a buried bone. My mother always complained of my insatiable curiosity, and my inability to keep that same nose out of other people's business, prophesying that it would do me no good.

'Very well,' I capitulated, 'I'll stay with you until spring if you'll have me. But you must accept payment for the past fortnight's lodging, and I'll not take no for an answer. I've sufficient money to support myself for several weeks, although some I must necessarily keep back to replenish my pack, which I can do easily enough from the cargo ships which tie up here at Redcliffe Wharf. On that condition, I'll stop.'

Although neither woman's face displayed the slightest sign of triumph, I could sense the relief in both of them; an easing of the tense lines around the mouth and a lightening of the brow.

'Tomorrow, I'll borrow a truckle bed from Nick Brimble,' Margaret said, plying her knife again and tossing chopped leek and turnip into the iron pot, where the water was beginning to bubble gently in the fire's heat.

I nodded, bowing to the inevitable. 'And this story you were going to tell me about your father?' I asked. I saw Margaret's lips tighten and added, 'Lillis is right. If I'm to live with you, it's as well I should know of any trouble. Others will make it their business to see that I do, even if you keep me in ignorance.'

'There you are, Mother!' Lillis gave me a blinding smile. 'Roger agrees with me, and it's only fair he should know what happened.'

Margaret hesitated before nodding a reluctant agreement. 'But we'll eat first. After supper, we can be cosy by the fire and no one likely to disturb us. There's a cutting wind blowing off the river and an icy sleet. Not a night for anyone to be about.' I wondered if she were thinking, as I was, of that mysterious nocturnal visit she had received so recently, but she gave no sign of unease. 'There, that's the last of the vegetables. The stew shouldn't take long now.'

The meal had been eaten and cleared away. The shutters were fastened against the unfriendly night, and the three of us drew close to the fire, whose fierce blaze had been banked down with turfs cut from neighbouring fields and sold from door to door by the turfer, who had called that same morning. At the time I had reflected, somewhat sententiously, how much city-dwellers had done for them which country folk had to do for themselves. Mistress Walker had no stock-cupboard worth mentioning, not even for the winter months, but went daily to the market for whatever was needful in the way of food. Her other wants were supplied by pedlars coming to the door; and when I asked what happened when heavy snowfalls or floods kept suppliers from reaching the city, I was told that the castle or the abbey or any of the many wealthy houses would hand out dried fish or grain. No one starved, although many might go hungry, in bad weather.

Lillis had brought my mattress as near to the hearth as she dared, and was curled up on it, more like a cat than ever. Margaret Walker and I sat on the two stools, supporting our backs when necessary against the table edge, but for the most part leaning towards the glowing warmth of the fire. Outside, the day's noise and bustle had dwindled to an occasional shout, a dog's bark and the distant call of the Watch as it patrolled the icy streets. Now and then, a bitter draught penetrated the smoke-blackened hole in the roof, bringing with it a spatter of rain, but we merely huddled closer to the heat.

While Margaret Walker searched for words with which to begin her story, I had time to study her. Lillis resembled her mother more closely than I had realized, for Margaret, too, was small and thin with large brown eyes which dominated her face, and the wisps of hair which strayed from beneath her hood were as black as her daughter's. But it was not just her added years which gave the impression of a greater maturity. There was a solidity and common sense about Margaret which I felt sure that Lillis would never achieve, and I could tell by the way the older woman kept a vigilant watch upon the younger that she also felt this way. There was something lacking in Lillis, a sense of responsibility, of morality, which made her seem almost fey.

'My father,' Margaret said abruptly, as though deciding that if she didn't speak now, she might change her mind altogether, 'died at the beginning of last month, some three or four weeks before Christmas. His name was William Woodward, and in his youth he was a weaver by trade.'

The story came out piecemeal, with interruptions from Lillis, questions from me, events omitted only to be recalled later and recounted out of place, or incidents recollected too soon, leading to involved explanations and recriminations from one at least of Margaret's listeners. So I will tell the story here as I came to understand it when her narrative was finished and I had had time to put the facts in order in my mind.

William Woodward had been born, during the last years of the reign of King Henry IV, into the close-knit weavers' community of Redcliffe in Bristol He had been apprenticed as a boy to Master Jocelyn Weaver, the head of one of the city's wealthiest families concerned in the cloth trade. William had lived for seven years in the Weaver household, as a good apprentice should, and, at the end of his time, had become a journeyman weaver. Unfortunately, when he had applied to join the Weavers' Guild, his masterpiece had been rejected as of inferior standard, and he had therefore been unable to set up in business on his own account, a state of affairs which he deeply resented. A grudging man, he had, I gathered, blamed his failure on everyone but himself and his own poor workmanship.

At the age of twenty-two or thereabouts – he was never quite sure of his exact age – he had married Jennifer Peto, a young Cornishwoman, who had travelled to Bristol with her parents a few years earlier. Of the couple's four children, only Margaret, the eldest and the only girl, survived infancy. Jennifer died when Margaret was in her middle twenties and Lillis some six years old. Margaret had dutifully taken her father to live with her and the child, for by then she herself was a widow.

In her nineteenth year, she had married, within the weaving community, Adam Walker; in her own words 'as good and kind a man as ever breathed.' Lillis had been born two years later and a son, Colin, a twelve-month after that. It needed no great skill to discern that this boy had been the apple of Margaret's eye, and I stole a sidelong glance at Lillis to see how she took such overt partiality. But her face was untroubled; and if she realized that her long-dead little brother still meant more to her mother than she did, she showed no sign of resentment.

Colin Walker was barely two years old when he accompanied his mother, one hot summer afternoon, to the weaving sheds to take his father a draught of cider. Adam had been allowed to the door to see and speak to his wife, and while his parents were talking, Colin strayed into the middle of the road, attracted by the debris sluggishly floating along the open drain. And it had been at that precise moment that a horse, harnessed to a cart loaded with bales of cloth, had been frightened by some passing urchins and bolted. The driver was drunk, having spent the previous hour in one of the local inns.

Adam Walker, who was facing the road, saw the danger to his son before his wife did, and hurled himself into the path of the oncoming horse and cart in a vain attempt to throw the boy clear. Both were killed, the child almost instantly, the father after lingering in agony for several hours. Margaret was left inconsolable and grief-stricken, mourning a husband whose memory was so potent that she could never bring herself to marry again. Alfred Weaver, who had by then inherited the business from his father, Jocelyn, and to whom the horse and cart belonged, had allowed Margaret and Lillis to remain in the cottage, which had been their home ever since.

And it was here, in this room where I now sat, that William Woodward, newly widowed, had joined his daughter and granddaughter in the summer of 1460; or, at least, I judged it to be so from Margaret's insistence that it was the year the Duke of York, father of King Edward, God bless him, returned from Ireland to lay claim to the throne, and was later killed at the battle at Wakefield. William was still a journeyman weaver, still disgruntled and less than grateful – or such was my guess – for the filial duty and attention heaped upon him.

He remained with Margaret and Lillis for well on nine years, and was already fast approaching the age when his daughter expected that she would have to support him as he grew too old to handle the heavy shuttles and looms, when William seemed to gain a new lease of life. He left weaving and the protection of Margaret's care, and went to live in a cottage in Bell Lane, near St John's Gate, the property of Edward Herepath, for whom he now worked. For this same Edward Herepath was the city's biggest landlord and had offered William Woodward employment as a rent and debt collector, when his former bailiff had left him to be married.

When she spoke of the circumstance, Margaret Walker's voice still registered the same sense of astonishment she had felt at the time.

'For you must know,' she said to me, 'that Father was not a young man. Big and well-built, I grant you – Lillis and I get our small bones from my mother – but grey-haired and not much short of his sixtieth year; an age when most men would be quietly and decently contemplating death. To change his trade like that at such an advanced time of life was something very few people could understand. And even less understandable was Edward Herepath's decision to employ him, for they were two men with little in common who had, as far as I knew, never exchanged words prior to this transaction.'

'Tell me about Edward Herepath,' I suggested.

Margaret added a few sticks to the fire before positioning a fresh turf to contain the blaze. 'I was going to,' she answered, 'for Edward Herepath and his brother Robert are at the very heart of this story. Indeed, without them, there would not be one.'

Edward Herepath, she informed me, was some thirty-five or -six years old, the elder of the two sons of Giles Herepath, wealthy soap manufacturer and respected burgess of the city, and his wife, Adela. When Edward was eighteen, his mother had died giving birth to her second child, Robert. A grieving Giles had followed his wife to the grave only two years later, leaving everything, including the upbringing of the infant Robert, to his elder son. Edward, who apparently had no interest in the manufacture of soap, had disposed of the business to a friend of his father, one Peter Avenel, and with the money thus obtained, bought up a number of properties in and around Bristol, which returned him a handsome profit in rents.

As far as the baby brother – with whom he had been

saddled at so young an age – was concerned, everyone agreed that his devotion was exemplary. Nothing that could make up for the lack of a mother and father had been denied Robert; his every wish had been his brother's command. Even when Edward married, no children of his own had come along to challenge Robert's supremacy in the household.

'With the result,' snorted Margaret, 'that you may well guess at. Robert grew from a wilful, spoilt child into an even wilder and unbiddable youth, a constant source of worry to his brother and, above all, a gambler, forever in debt.'

'But handsome,' sighed Lillis, a predatory light gleaming in her cat-like eyes. 'One of the best-looking young men in the city.'

'Oh, I don't deny that,' agreed her mother. 'And to give him his due, I don't believe he was aware of, or even cared about, his looks or the effect they had on women. Leastways, not until Cicely Ford came on the scene.'

'Cicely Ford?' I queried, storing away yet another name in my memory and wondering where the story was leading me.

'A truly beautiful girl,' Margaret said with decision. 'Beautiful by nature as well as in person.' Lillis gave a little sniff, but did not contradict her mother's description. Margaret went on. 'Her father, John Ford, was one of the wealthiest burgesses of this city. He was an exporter of soap, wine, cloth; anything you care to name. He owned nine ships and employed above eight hundred souls. His merchant's mark, they say, was known the length and breadth of Europe. And one of his ships, the *Cicely*, was part of an expedition that sailed westwards to find the great Western Isles men talk about, the islands of Brazil. But storms turned the ships back some way off the Irish coast.'

She sat a moment, staring into the heart of the fire, lost in contemplation of those lands far out in the Atlantic Ocean; those fabled shores which sailors used to swear they had glimpsed, or knew of some other ship's crew which had almost made landfall on them. (Nowadays, of course, we know that they are there, those strange, far-off lands peopled by red-skinned men. The Italian, Christopher Columbus, and Bristol's own Venetian adventurers, Giovanni Cabot and his son Sebastian, have set foot in them.)

The resin of a twig caught flame and sent up a shower of sparks. Margaret Walker jumped and laughed. 'I was day-dreaming,' she said. 'I've forgotten where I was. What point in the story had I reached?'

'You were singing the praises of Mistress Ford,' her daughter answered drily. 'The perfect, the ever-lovely Cicely.'

'And so she is!' Margaret declared roundly. 'One of the kindest, sweetest, prettiest, most devout ladies to grace this earth.' I had – then – reservations that anyone could be so perfect, but I held my tongue and allowed my hostess to continue uninterrupted.

It seemed that Master John Ford had died of a sudden

apoplexy four years previously, leaving Cicely, his only child, orphaned, Dame Ford having departed this life some time earlier. John Ford had been a close friend in his youth of Giles Herepath, and had always deeply admired Edward, the elder son. And in spite of what might have been seen as Edward's mishandling of his brother, Robert, Master Ford had nonetheless left Cicely to Edward's care for the remaining years of her minority, trusting, no doubt, in his ability to handle her vast fortune with the same skill with which he managed his own business affairs.

'And Master Edward's wife was a sober, decorous woman,' Margaret told me, 'a great benefactress of the Church and altogether a fitting preceptress for such a girl as Cicely Ford.'

'And constantly ailing,' Lillis put in; her high-pitched tones, sharp as a needle, stabbing the momentary silence.

Her mother glanced reprovingly at her. 'Are you suggesting, Miss, that she was shamming?' Margaret turned to me. 'Many people thought that during her lifetime, but they had to eat their words. The poor lady died in her thirtieth year, less than nine months after Cicely went to live in the Herepath house in Small Street.'

Chapter Four

A flurry of hailstones rattled the shutters and fell through the hole in the roof to hiss among the burning twigs and sea coal, sending a thin column of smoke towards the ceiling. Margaret placed another turf on the fire, while Lillis sat upright on the mattress, pulling one of the blankets about her shoulders. The room had grown chilly and I was glad of my leather jerkin, lined with scarlet, which had been given me in exchange for goods by a widow who had fallen on lean times. It had belonged to her husband, and the warm, cochineal-dyed wool helped preserve my bodily warmth as it had once done his.

'So,' I said, 'Edward Herepath found himself again saddled with the responsibility of a minor, this time a young girl and not of his blood. What did he do about it?'

'He hired a good, sensible woman of the town to be Cicely's companion, and probably hoped that the girl's influence would have an improving effect upon his brother.'

'And did it?'

Margaret shook her head. 'Not a whit. Robert carried on his reprehensible way just as before. But . . .' and here she paused significantly, 'he fell in love with her. What is more, Cicely fell in love with him.'

'And yet she held no sway over him?'

'None whatsoever. He continued drinking and gambling and idling away his days, and still she would look at no other man. It seemed that nothing he did gave her a disgust of him. I have no doubt that many people tried to persuade her to give him up, especially as there were so many other young men anxious for her favours. Everyone knows that Robin Avenel, whose father bought the Herepath soap-works, is mad for love of her, and has been for many a long day. She tried to influence Robert, of course, but her gentle persuasions fell on deaf ears and, much as he loved her – or said he loved her – he never even attempted to please her in that way.'

'How do you know all this?' I asked curiously.

Margaret shrugged. 'How does anyone get to know such things? Gossip gets around, in the market-place, in the shops. Dame Freda, Cicely's companion, told friends, who told other friends, who were overheard talking by their servants.' She smiled. 'If you're thinking I might have received the information from my father, you're wrong. The one person I could reasonably have expected to give me details of the Herepaths was the one person who took no interest in them. But then, my father was incurious about the day-to-day lives of his fellow human beings. His only interest was in the state of their souls.'

'He was a pious man?'

Margaret's lips thinned until they were almost invisible. 'Oh, yes,' she answered shortly.

Lillis looked up from the huddle of blankets. 'When my father and little brother were killed, Mother's faith was sorely tested.'

Margaret glanced uneasily across her shoulder, as though afraid someone might be listening. 'Hold your tongue, girl! Do you want me accused of heresy? Not,' she added, turning to me, 'that it isn't partly the truth. Since Adam and Colin died, I have had difficulty in believing in a just and merciful God. I've confessed it to my parish priest and he assures me that faith will come back if I pray for it. When I point out that it is almost seventeen years since they died, he says either that I am not praying hard enough or that I am not sufficiently contrite for my backsliding. Either way, it is my fault and not God's, and of course he's right.'

'No he's not,' Lillis said fiercely, her strange cat's eyes glowing in the firelight. 'A God of love wouldn't allow such things to happen.'

'Hush, hush, you stupid child!' Margaret exclaimed in an agony of apprehension. 'Do you want to bring more trouble down upon our heads than we have already? You shouldn't say such things in front of Roger.'

Lillis gave her small, secret smile. 'I trust him,' she replied calmly. The childish upper lip curled to reveal her little white, very even teeth. 'He has doubts sometimes, too.'

39

I stared at her in consternation. How in Heaven's name did she know that? No word on the subject had ever passed between us. Was she a witch? Had she supernatural powers that she could read the secret places of my heart? Or was it that she simply had an instinctive ability to draw the right conclusions from little things that people said or did? I could never make up my mind with Lillis.

I said hurriedly: 'You may trust me, at all events, to keep your confidence.' I avoided a further glance in Lillis's direction and continued, 'You were talking, Mistress Walker, about Robert Herepath and Cicely Ford.'

She nodded, relieved to turn the conversation away from dangerous topics. 'I was, although there is little else to add on that score.' She took a deep breath and settled herself more comfortably on her stool, leaning forward to hold her hands to the slumbering fire. 'Now we come to the heart of the story, to the strange happenings which began on Lady Day of last year and only ended with the death of my father before Christmas. Although to say the tale is ended is wishful thinking on my part, for until the mystery is resolved there will never be an end, not for me and Lillis, nor for Edward Herepath and Cicely Ford. Lillis, there's small ale in the jug on the table. Pour Roger a cup while I get on with the story.'

Lillis did as her mother bade her, then returned to her seat on the mattress and once again burrowed inside my blankets, like a small animal going to ground. Her eyes gleamed at me from inside the cave of rough wool she had fashioned around herself. I looked away quickly and concentrated on Mistress Walker.

'It began on the day of Our Lady's Annunciation, last March,' she said. 'The day my father collected all the outstanding rents and debts owed to Edward Herepath for the quarter.'

On that particular Quarter Day, Edward Herepath had arranged to visit Gloucester to look over a horse he intended to buy from the acquaintance of a friend. Because of the length of journey involved, he decided to remain in the city for two nights, travelling to Gloucester on the Thursday, inspecting his prospective purchase on the Friday and, taking his leisure, returning to Bristol on Saturday. As a consequence of this, he had asked William Woodward to keep the money safe in his own cottage in Bell Lane, rather than delivering it to Small Street.

'For although he may have trusted his servants,' Margaret Walker said, 'he didn't trust his brother not to get his hands on the money somehow or other. Or part of it, at least. For everyone knew that Robert was heavily in debt to one or two of his cronies at the White Hart in Broad Street, where they played dicing games nearly every evening.'

Margaret, however, had known nothing of this arrangement when, on the Saturday morning, she had set out to visit her father in Bell Lane. She had not seen him on the Friday, but there were often occasions when she had no knowledge of his movements for several days together.

'We had little in common,' she told me in a low voice,

'and were never eager to seek out one another's company after he left the shelter of this roof. But I did my duty as a daughter and visited him regularly to make sure that he was eating properly and had his necessary share of comfort.'

But on the morning of Saturday 27 March, she had been totally unprepared for what she would find.

'I knocked at the street door, but got no reply, so I tried the latch. It was nearing mid-morning by then, and my father, if he were at home, would have been up and about, so I was not uneasy at being able to walk straight in. There was no sign of Father, however, and the first thing I noticed was that the door of a small wall cupboard, which he normally kept locked and in which he kept his few items of any value, was swinging open: its lock had been forced. But the silver-handled knife which his mother left him, and which had been passed down from generation to generation in his family, and an enamelled belt buckle and Cornish loving spoon which were my mother's, were still there. For a moment I assumed he had lost the key to the cupboard and forced the lock himself.'

But Margaret soon had cause to change her opinion. When she began to look around her, she was horrified to notice what looked like dried bloodstains among the rushes on the floor and on her father's bedding. The bed, moreover, had been left unmade, an unusual omission on William Woodward's part, for he was, so Margaret assured me, meticulous in his domestic habits and hated slovenliness in all its forms. A search of the cottage, including a visit to the outside privy, convinced his daughter that something was seriously wrong, and inquiries of his neighbours elicited the information that no one remembered seeing him since late on Thursday afternoon, when he had been noticed by one of them coming out of the butcher's shop near All Hallow's Church, where he had obviously bought some meat to cook for his supper. A whole day and two nights had passed without any knowledge of William's whereabouts.

'To cut a long story short,' Margaret continued, 'I called in the Watch, who informed the sheriff. Two of his officers began at once to investigate the affair, but there was no light shed on the matter until Master Herepath returned from Gloucester that same afternoon.'

Edward had wasted no time, but immediately gone in search of William Woodward and his money. It was then that the meaning of the forced cupboard door had become apparent, and questions were asked as to who, apart from Edward himself, had known that William was holding the rents. In the end, with great reluctance, the elder Herepath admitted that he had inadvertently let the information slip to his brother.

Margaret stirred, moving her face back from the fire, as though it had suddenly become too warm for her, yet at the same time wrapping her arms about her body as if she were cold.

'The two leather bags which had contained the money, and what was left of the coin itself after he had paid his ·

most pressing debts, were found in Robert Herepath's room in Small Street,' she said quietly. 'Robert freely admitted to taking the money, relying, I suppose, on his brother's goodwill not to bring charges against him, but denied all knowledge of my father. His story was that he had gone to Bell Lane after curfew, intending to knock up my father and spin him a tale of Edward changing his mind at the last minute, and asking him instead to collect and hold the money at Small Street until Edward's return. However, on Robert's arrival at the cottage, he had been unable to get any reply to his knocking, but had discovered, as I had done, that the door was unbolted; so he had lifted the latch and crept in.'

Robert Herepath, sensing that the cottage was empty, and presuming that William Woodward had slipped out for a while about some business of his own, had hurriedly drawn the dagger from his belt and prised open the door of the wall cupboard, guessing, from prior experience of the Bell Lane house, that it would be the most likely place for the money to be stored. He was not disappointed and, having extracted it, made off round the corner to Small Street as fast as he could, latching the street door behind him. The theft had been carried out in darkness and he had therefore been unable to take note of his surroundings. Of the fact that violence appeared to have been done there, he disclaimed all knowledge. Such had been Robert Herepath's story and he never wavered from it, Margaret said, even at the end.

And that end had come three months later, on a June

day of high summer, at the end of a hangman's rope.

'Robert Herepath was hanged for your father's murder?' I asked, sitting bolt upright and frowning. 'But . . . But surely you have told me more than once that Master Woodward died just before Christmas, here, in this cottage.'

Margaret nodded slowly, her eyes fixed on the heart of the fire. 'That is so. For you see, two months after the hanging, on the Day of the Assumption of Our Lady, Father walked back into Bristol, alive, although far from well.'

Robert had been under suspicion for the murder of William Woodward almost from the moment he admitted to stealing his brother's rents. Dried blood had been discovered on the outside of one of the leather pouches and smeared over the left breast of his jerkin, where, presumably, he had cradled the bags in his left arm. Several days later, William's bloodstained hat had been fished out of the River Frome by two young boys, angling for the family supper. The presumption was that his body had been pitched into the water just beyond St John's Archway, on the townward side of the Frome Gate.

Margaret Walker raised a hand to her forehead and held it there for several seconds, her eyes closed, as though trying to block out the events which followed. But at last, she lowered her hand again and went on: 'A strange kind of madness seemed to grip the town. Robert Herepath had made too many enemies in his time, for he was arrogant as well as spendthrift, and now suddenly everyone saw a chance for revenge; all those he had deliberately insulted or simply offended by his thoughtlessness, all those he owed money to and had never repaid, and all those young men who wanted Cicely Ford for themselves and saw a possibility of getting her if once Robert was out of the way. I don't say that people set out to tell lies, but they began to convince themselves that they had heard and seen things which we now know they couldn't have done. At Robert's trial, there were witnesses who swore to hearing cries and moans coming from Father's cottage the night he disappeared; one of them declared he had looked from his window in the small hours of the morning and was convinced that he had seen a shadowy figure fumbling at the wicket gate next to St John's Archway which gives on to the Frome Quay. Even Cicely Ford turned against Robert and refused to see him while he was in prison or even before he was hanged.' Margaret shuddered. 'I tell you, it was as though some evil possessed us all, willing Robert Herepath's destruction. There was no body, yet the jury found him guilty. No one heeded his protestations of innocence.'

She was growing agitated and I leaned across and gently squeezed her arm. 'You are speaking with the knowledge of hindsight,' I said. 'At the time, the evidence must have pointed strongly to his having murdered your father. If your father's body had been pitched into the Frome, as the evidence suggested, then it could have been borne down-river into the Avon and thence out to sea on the tide. And Robert had admitted to taking the money; the rest followed naturally. In addition, there were witnesses who persuaded themselves they had seen and heard things which you now know they could not have done. But the jury did not know that at the time.' There was a pause before I asked, 'After your father came back, what happened?'

Margaret bit her lip. 'I was sitting here, spinning. It was the Day of the Assumption of Our Lady and a beautiful, warm August afternoon. I was alone because Lillis had gone to fetch more wool from the dyer's, and I recall that I was humming a tune. I was beginning to get over what I believed to be Father's death and the subsequent horror of Robert Herepath's trial and execution. Life was getting back to normal again. The door was open as it was so hot, and I remember the noise of some children playing in the street; half a dozen boys trying to kick a blown swine's bladder between two posts.' She drew a deep breath. 'I was watching my wheel, teasing out a snag of wool from the spindle, when a shadow fell across the threshold.'

She had thought nothing of it; many people called at the cottage in the course of a day, and she had glanced up, smiling a welcome. But the smile had turned to an incredulous stare, which had rapidly changed to one of horrified disbelief. For standing in the open doorway was her father. William Woodward, for whose murder another man had been tried, found guilty and hanged, was still alive.

Or half alive. According to Margaret, her father was a

mere shadow of his former self; a broken man whose memory played him constant tricks, the result of some great blows to the head, the healed scars of which were plainly visible on his forehead and on the scalp beneath his thinning grey hair. He never again recovered his former good health or wanted to set foot out of doors, spending the short time remaining to him sitting crouched over the fire, which he seemed to need whatever the weather.

'But what did he say had happened to him?' I asked. 'Where had he been for those missing months between March and August? Was he able to tell you?'

Margaret shrugged despairingly. 'All that I or the sheriff's officers could get out of him, after many hours of questioning, was that he had been captured by slavers and carried to Ireland. Beyond that, there was no sense to be had of him.'

'But might that not have been the truth?' I knew that the slave trade between Bristol and Dublin had been outlawed for many centuries, but it was still carried on. Like the smuggling of other contraband merchandise, it throve in the dark.

Margaret raised her head and looked me full in the eyes. There were shadows beneath her own. 'He was an old man,' she said, 'past sixty. Why would slavers bother with him, however strong and hearty, a man with a respectable family and an employer who would raise the hue and cry if he vanished, when there are so many younger people who either have no home, or whose parents are willing to sell them into slavery? Young people give good value for money to the purchaser. An old man like my father would hardly be worth the cost of his passage to Ireland.'

Chapter Five

A profound quiet settled over the room, in which the sudden cry of the Watch from an adjoining street sounded as loudly as if they had been in there with us. I know Margaret and I both jumped, but there was never a stir from Lillis.

It was she, however, who broke the silence, referring back to her mother's last remark. 'It's what everyone thinks, including the sheriff's men and the sheriff himself, for all I know.'

Margaret shivered. 'It's true. No one believed my father's story, and although some had the sense to accept that he was not responsible for what he was saying – that he was confused and befuddled in his wits – there were many more who thought that he was covering his tracks for some evil doings of his own.' She once more pressed a hand to her forehead. 'And who's to condemn the poor souls if they wanted to shift their own guilt on to Father? When people remembered what their words and testimony had done to Robert Herepath, even if they had not actually borne witness at his trial, is it any wonder that they needed someone else to blame?'

'That may be so,' Lillis responded drily from among her blankets, 'but when he died, they began looking askance at us, as though we too are not telling them all we know.'

'Is this true?' I inquired of Margaret.

She nodded. 'Oh, we have friends, real friends like Nick Brimble, to see we come to no harm. But there are those who won't give us the time of day, and shopkeepers who refuse to serve us.'

I snorted contemptuously. 'What of Edward Herepath and Mistress Ford? How do they treat you?'

'Well enough,' Margaret conceded. 'What bitterness and anger they feel, they don't lay at our door, although Edward Herepath could never bring himself to visit Father. But Mistress Cicely came on several occasions, latterly bringing him broth from the Small Street kitchen when she saw how ill he was. She blames no one more than she blames herself for denying belief in Robert's story. She has grown so thin and pale and silent these past few months that it breaks my heart to see her.'

Lillis mumbled something under her breath which I was unable to catch, nor did I wish to. She would have little sympathy with anyone's sorrows but her own and, to do her justice, even those would receive short shrift. She was not a girl who indulged in self-pity. Any display of sympathy on my part for the two women's predicament would be ill-received by her, but I felt that Mistress Walker was in need of friendship.

'I can see that things are difficult for you,' I said. 'People find it hard to blame themselves for any tragedy, and need a scapegoat. But can you think of no reason for your father's absence? A reason which would take into account the bloodstains you found in the Bell Lane cottage? It still seems to me that his story is the only one which explains all the circumstances.'

I was not looking at Lillis, but I heard the sound of an indrawn breath, as though she were about to speak. Margaret cut in firmly, 'No, nothing.' Was she just a little too vehement? 'I am sure in my own mind, however, that he was not taken to Ireland for the reasons I have told you. And Alderman Weaver, who has many contacts in Waterford and Dublin, has made inquiries for me insofar as he may, but no one recollects having seen hide nor hair of my father.'

'Alderman Weaver?' I asked, my attention momentarily diverted. 'Who lives in Broad Street?' But of course she had mentioned an Alfred Weaver earlier in connection with her husband. I should have realized then of whom she was speaking. He was the owner of many of the weaving sheds this side of the Avon. When she nodded, puzzled, I went on, 'I have some acquaintance with him. Indeed two years ago I was able to do him a service in connection with the disappearance of his son. I'll tell you of it sometime, but it's too long a story to be gone into here and now. Suffice it to say that, with his blessing, I could probably inquire further into this business if that is really what you want.'

Both women were half inclined to probe more deeply

into my connections with Alderman Weaver, but thankfully their own concerns were uppermost in their minds and they soon abandoned their half-hearted questioning.

'If there is indeed anything that you can discover, it would be a relief to know it,' Margaret said, 'for at least it might prove that Lillis and I had no knowledge of whatever, or whoever, it was lured Father from home that night and inflicted on him such terrible injuries.' But there was a note of doubt in her voice, as though she were aware that the truth is not always pleasant.

Lillis had no such misgivings. 'We need to know anything Roger can find out, Mother, in spite of the fact it might besmirch Grandfather's good name. He must be told everything.'

Margaret rose to her feet and placed two more turfs on the fire, banking it right down for the night ahead, so that no stray spark could set the cottage aflame. What was left of the earlier blaze might smoulder until morning, or go out altogether in the cold night hours, in which case it would have to be relit on the morrow.

'Roger knows all that you or I can tell him,' she answered smoothly, yet I also detected a hint of warning behind her words. 'If we remember aught that we've forgotten, it will be time enough then to repair the omission but, for now, we're all three tired and need our beds. Lillis, get up from that mattress and straighten the blankets and move it back against the wall.' When her daughter had done her bidding, Margaret pulled the curtain of faded red and green woven fabric which divided the room in two, smiled her good-nights and vanished with Lillis behind its shelter. 'Sleep well,' she called out as she got into bed.

I stripped to my shirt and rolled between the blankets, nestling my head on the soft, feather-filled pillow. I was still weak after my illness and aching in every limb with weariness, but sleep eluded me. I tossed, restless and uneasy, from side to side, going over in my mind the strange facts of William Woodward's disappearance. That he had been removed from home by force seemed obvious, or why else would there have been bloodstains? And Margaret had spoken of scars which showed injuries to his head which would account for them. Furthermore, the discovery of his hat in the River Frome would make sense if he had indeed been dragged aboard a ship bound for Ireland. And in that case, the evidence of witnesses who said they had heard screams and moans coming from William's cottage, or seen shadowy figures by St John's Wicket, need not be discounted.

There appeared, however, to be too much doubt by too many people on this score for me to insist on its being the likeliest explanation, and until I had spoken to Alderman Weaver, I must reserve judgement. I would visit him tomorrow morning, and trust that he would let me presume on our former acquaintance to give me audience. Meantime, what other answer could there be to the riddle of William's apparent death and mysterious resurrection? And why did I have a strange, nagging feeling at the back of my mind that Margaret Walker was keeping something from me? With these and other unresolved questions circling inside my head, I at last fell into a troubled sleep and woke in the morning, still weary.

I knew I should give myself a few more days' rest before undertaking any great exertion, but I trusted to my natural strength and rude health to see me through my investigations. For the truth was that, in spite of having agreed to be the Walkers' lodger for what was left of the winter months, I was anxious to pay my debt and be free of them. It was not that I disliked either woman; indeed, I already felt the stirrings of affection for Margaret Walker because she reminded me in some ways of my mother. It was Lillis who made me uneasy. The determined and predatory glint which appeared in her eyes whenever they glanced my way, told me that I was a marked man and that she would snare me if she could. She was twenty years of age, for all that she looked younger, and ripe for a husband.

I rose before the two women were even stirring, pulled on my hose, unlatched the door and walked down the narrow alley alongside the cottage to the yard at the back. When I had used the privy, I fetched up water from the well which served the surrounding cottages, poured some over my head, filled a tin can and carried it indoors. A judicious use of the bellows brought the slumbering fire to life, and when I had removed the turfs I was able to heat my shaving water and get rid of my beard. I had lit two of the rushlights, trusting that their fragile glow would disturb neither Margaret nor Lillis for a while, but I hoped in vain. As I ran a satisfied hand over my once again smooth chin, Lillis slid out from behind the curtain.

She was wearing nothing but her thin linen shift and, as I turned my head to look at her, she lifted her arms, stretching and yawning, smiling secretively and watching me between half-closed lids.

'You're handsomer without a beard,' she said, 'if that's possible.'

I made no reply. What was there to say? I was not a vain youth, but neither was I falsely modest. I knew women found me good-looking, and had often marvelled that Nature should have endowed me in such a way; for my father, what I remembered of him, was a small dark man with weather-beaten features. My mother always maintained that I was a throwback to her grandfather. 'A true Saxon,' she used to call him. She herself was fair, but her hair was more honey-gold than mine, and her eyes less intensely blue.

'I'll get more water,' I offered, 'to boil the oatmeal for breakfast,' and, lifting the can from the fire, I was about to retreat into the yard, when Lillis moved swiftly to block my passage to the door.

'Are you afraid of me?' she asked, her mouth tilting into a provocative grin.

'Why should I be?' I asked, praying that Margaret would come to my rescue, and sensing that, if she did not, it would be only a matter of moments before those thin, childish arms were wound around my neck and the thin but sensuous body was pressed against mine.

For once my prayer was speedily answered. Although my back was to the curtain which divided the room, I knew that Margaret had emerged from behind it by the change of expression on her daughter's face. The look of naked desire faded abruptly to be replaced by a sullen pout, and the narrow shoulders were visibly braced for Margaret's reprimand.

'Lillis! Get dressed immediately! Suppose someone were to walk in, what would they think? There's enough gossip about us already, without you adding fuel to the flames.'

Breakfast – oatmeal and dried fish – was not a comfortable meal, with Lillis sulky and out of humour, and Margaret preoccupied, plainly wondering if she had invited trouble beneath her roof when she had urged me to stay. I, too, was worrying about the same thing. My best course, I decided yet again, was to find out what I could about William Woodward's disappearance and then take my leave. I eyed my chapman's pack with longing, suppressing the desire to grab it and run.

Margaret must have followed my glance, for I turned my head to see her watching me anxiously. I gave her a reassuring smile. 'I'll be off to Broad Street as soon as it's light,' I promised.

I approached Alderman Weaver's house in Broad Street as I had done two years ago, from the back and the narrow confines of Tower Lane. The little walled garden with its pear and apple trees, both now bare of leaves, its herb and flower beds deep in their winter slumber, was much as I remembered it. But the formidable dame with the bunch of keys at her belt who came to the kitchen door in answer to my knock, was not Marjorie Dyer. She, I supposed, had long gone.

My request to speak to the Alderman was greeted with suspicion, and my insistence that he would know me with outright contempt. Behind the housekeeper's back, I could see two little kitchen-maids regarding me goggle-eyed, delighted by the unexpected diversion. I was desperately calculating how long it would be before the door was slammed in my face with nothing achieved, when someone entered the garden and made to push past me into the warmth of the kitchen.

'Ned!' I exclaimed thankfully. 'Ned Stoner! I must see the Alderman. Tell the goodwife here that he knows me.'

The heavy, lantern-jawed face regarded me straitly for a moment, then was wreathed in smiles. 'Dang me, if it ain't the chapman! How goes it then, me old acker? What you doing back in Bristol?' And without waiting for an answer to either of these questions, he addressed himself to the dragon barring my path. 'It's all right, Dame Judith, you can tell the master 'e's here. The master'll see 'im, too, I shouldn't wonder. Owes our friend the chapman a lot, I reckon.'

Stiff with outraged dignity, the housekeeper eventually withdrew, reappearing some minutes later to say that Alderman Weaver would indeed be pleased to see me.

Her reluctance at delivering this message was aggravated by the sight of me, at Ned's invitation, already inside her kitchen, and the two girls neglecting their duties to stare and giggle bashfully. She was plainly at a loss to account for my standing with her master, and I speculated whether or not she would sink her pride sufficiently to question Ned about it after I was gone.

The alderman had finished his breakfast and received me in the parlour with its painted and carved doorposts and roof-beams. The glass windows, which had so intrigued me when I first saw them, were dulled now with the grime of winter, but still let in a deal of light. The ornate cupboard, displaying the family pewter and silver-ware, had been removed to another corner from the one in which it previously stood but, apart from that, all was much as it had been. The alderman, rising to greet me from one of the armchairs beside the hearth, on which burned a roaring fire, was as I remembered him; a little older, perhaps, a little more careworn, the hair sparser and greyer, but with the same thickset build and old-fashioned clothes.

He held out his hand in greeting and waved me to the other armchair. 'Roger Chapman,' he said, 'how can I help you?'

I explained my errand and, as I did so, a faint smile, tinged with sadness, curved his lips.

'So,' he said, when at last I finished speaking, 'you are still using your peculiar talent to help other people as you once helped me. With,' he added, after a moment's

sorrowful reflection, 'the prospect of no happier an outcome. Less happy, perhaps, for at least I had the satisfaction of seeing the malefactors brought to justice. I fear
in this case, there is no hope of that, for the simple reason
that the crime lies at the door of us, the citizens of Bristol.
We allowed our dislike of a young man to cloud our
judgement; even, in some cases, making up evidence
against him and, worse still, growing to believe it, because
we wanted to think him guilty. A shame most of us will
have to bear for the rest of our lives.' He flung up a hand.
'Oh, I can guess what you're thinking; that what happened
to him did not make Robert Herepath any the less of a
burden to his brother and to the rest of us who had to
endure his effrontery, his gambling, his debts and drunk-
enness. But no man, whatever his faults, deserves to
choke to death at the end of a rope for a murder he did
not commit.'

I nodded. 'I think so, too. But I do *not* think that two
innocent women should be made to suffer for something
which was not their fault. Which is why I should like to
discover, if I'm able, where William Woodward was
during the time between March and August last year;
between the Day of the Annunciation and the Day of the
Assumption of Our Lady.'

The alderman frowned. 'An impossible task, I should
have thought, now that the only person who might have
thrown any light on the subject is dead.'

'He claimed to have been taken to Ireland by the
slavers, but no one seems to have believed him. Yet the

evidence of the hat, and of the witnesses at Robert Herepath's trial, would give the claim credence. Why is it so summarily dismissed?'

Alderman Weaver sighed. 'Because the slavers do not in general trouble themselves with people over a certain age; they are of little value in the market-place. But if they do – and there are unscrupulous men and women who will pay handsomely to be rid of elderly relatives – they are not so foolish as to beat the victim so severely about the head as to make him lose his wits. What profit would there be for them in that? No, the truth behind William's disappearance must be sought elsewhere. And now, young man, you must hold me excused. I have to be at the weaving sheds this morning. The aulnager is coming to inspect a consignment of cloth before it's dispatched to London and the Steelyard.'

Chapter Six

The alderman would have risen to his feet, but I stretched out a hand. 'A few minutes more of your time, Your Honour, I beg you.'

He hesitated, then sank back into his chair, but his manner betrayed impatience.

I went on quickly, 'Forgive me, but do you have certain knowledge that William Woodward's story was false?'

It was Alderman Weaver's turn to pause for thought, but after a moment, he said firmly, 'I do not have certain knowledge, no. That would be impossible. But if you ask me am I as sure as I can be, then the answer must be yes.' He sighed. 'I have often wished that Mistress Walker would marry again, but as she has never seemed inclined to do so, I have felt in some sense responsible for her and her daughter. Although nearly a score of years ago, it was one of my carters, a drunken fellow who should have been dismissed long before, who was the cause of her husband's death, and also that of her child. Her only son.' There was a poignant silence, during which I guessed he was thinking not of Colin Walker, but of his own son, Clement. The alderman continued bravely: 'Therefore, when this trouble came upon them; when William Woodward came back, as it were, from the dead, I felt obliged to investigate his story in the hope that it might prove to be true. If it were, then no blame could be attached to either him or his family.' He raised his earnest glance to mine and leaned slightly forward in his chair. 'I have done much business over the years with the Irish of the eastern seaboard, from Waterford up as far as Dublin, which is the trading ground of Bristol men. Many of these acquaintances have become good friends, for the Irish are a friendly people.'

'I doubt if those sold into slavery to them think so,' I put in drily.

The alderman smiled. 'In most cases you would be wrong. Oh, there are cruel masters, I don't deny. What nation can claim to be free of cruelty? But in general, the Irish treat their servants as friends, all sitting down to table together and eating from the same dish. You look incredulous, as well you might, but I assure you that it's true. I have seen it with my own eyes and know it to be the general custom. Many Bristol men and women, sold into slavery in Ireland, have found a happiness there they did not know at home. And although,' he added hastily, 'I cannot condone something that is a crime against both Church and State, its consequences are not always to be deplored.'

Realizing that my remark had caused him to digress, I

prompted, 'So you made inquiries of your Irish friends regarding William Woodward?'

'I did indeed, and very thorough they were, too. But no sighting of anyone resembling him could be recollected in any of the slave markets held in March last year. These markets of necessity take place in secret, but are well attended; and if my immediate informant had not been present, he always knew of someone else who had.' Alderman Weaver leaned even closer, thumping the arm of his chair. 'I feel sure in my own mind that an elderly man with severe head injuries would not have been overlooked, if only for the simple reason that his appearance would have provoked ridicule from the onlookers. Furthermore, there appears to have been no talk of a runaway slave in the latter half of August, and I am assured that such news does get about.' His gaze became yet more earnest. 'Mistress Walker has doubtless told you in what condition her father returned to her, and indeed, I saw William for myself on more than one occasion. The blows he had received to his head had addled his wits; and while I believe a man in his state could, by instinct, make his way home on foot, I am extremely doubtful of his having the ability to find a ship's master willing to transport him across water. Sailors are too superstitious. And if he *had* found someone, William had no money with which to pay for his passage.'

I realized with dismay that I had given very little thought to William Woodward's return journey, and silently upbraided myself for the lapse. This latter argument of the alderman seemed to me a more telling one than any he had hitherto advanced, although taken altogether, his reasoning convinced me that I must look elsewhere for the truth concerning the old man's disappearance. It seemed unlikely that he had ever been in Ireland.

I stood up. 'Thank you for your time and patience,' I murmured humbly, still shaken by the fact that I had obtained but half a story from Margaret Walker, and determined to remedy this omission as soon as possible. My recent illness, I decided, must have blunted the sharpness of my mind. The alderman also rose, anxious to be away to the weaving sheds and the waiting aulnager. I went on, 'If I am to help Mistress Walker discover what really happened to her father, I shall need to make more inquiries. But I hesitate to intrude upon the grief of Edward Herepath and Mistress Ford without some kind of introduction. Would you . . . could you provide me with a letter?'

Alderman Weaver considered my request, then nodded briskly. 'Accompany me to the weaving sheds, and I'll dictate some lines to my clerk after I have finished with the aulnager. Meantime, you can take yourself down to the tenter ground. It was two of the tenterers' children who fished William's hat from the Frome. You may gain some further information from them, although after all this time, I would not wish to raise false hopes. But something new may be discovered.'

He called for his manservant to bring his hat and warm frieze cloak, and together we set out, along Broad Street, down High Street, and across the bridge with its shops and tall, narrow houses. Spanning the middle of the bridge was a chapel dedicated to the Virgin and, as we passed through, I sent up a prayer, asking Our Lady's blessing on my mission. I might have asked for its successful conclusion, except I had learned at an early age that neither God, nor His gracious Lady Mother, nor His Son, our Saviour, are prepared to give something for nothing. I should have to work to ensure a happy outcome.

The weaving sheds were busy at that time of day, and the clack of the looms could be heard even before we reached St Thomas's Church. From every cottage there sounded the hum of spinning-wheels. The aulnager was already waiting outside the counting-house, tapping an impatient foot and resisting the head weaver's attempts to placate him for the alderman's tardiness. An alderman of Bristol, however, was unlikely to be intimidated by the annoyance of a mere city inspector, and Alderman Weaver took much longer than was necessary instructing me how to reach the tenter grounds, which lay on the other side of the Redcliffe wall, along the bank of the Avon.

'Come back later,' he told me finally, 'and you shall have your letter.'

I thanked him and went out by the Redcliffe Gate. To my left, William Canynges's beautiful church of St Mary stood guard over the row of houses climbing Redcliffe Hill, but I turned to my right, past the gravel pits to where the fullers had their small community, soaking and hammering the newly woven cloth before dispatching it to the tenters to be stretched. The tenter fields were further on again, looking across the river towards the Great Marsh and the Backs, where ships rode at anchor, waiting to be relieved of their cargoes or loaded for the journey home.

I cursed myself for a second time when I realized I had failed to ask the alderman for the two boys' names, but set about remedying the omission. There were a number of men working at the wooden frames. One couple near me fixed the selvedge of a piece of fulled cloth to the tenterhooks of the crossbar, before hooking the other selvedge to an even heavier wooden bar which was then allowed to swing free, its weight pulling and stretching the wet material into shape. When they had finished, I approached them cautiously and made my request. I knew from experience how loath closely knit communities of craftsmen were to give information to prying strangers, and was not surprised to be met with tightly shut mouths and uncomprehending stares. But once I had mentioned the names of Margaret Walker and Alderman Weaver, I was treated with less suspicion, and one of the two men told me what I needed to know.

'You're wanting Burl Hodge's young lads,' he said, giving me a long hard look. 'Come to think of it, Burl's mentioned you. You're the chapman who was taken sick some weeks back, just after Christmas. He helped carry you to Widow Walker's cottage, if I remember rightly.'

I assured him that he did and asked where I could find Burl Hodge's sons this time of day.

'You'd best ask Burl himself,' my informant answered

grudgingly, and nodded towards the opposite end of the field. 'Over there, with the green jerkin and brown hood.'

I thanked him and made my way between the frames to where Burl Hodge was taking a well-earned rest from the rigours of hanging wet cloth on a cold, dank January day. He regarded my approach with some suspicion until sudden recognition dawned. He stopped blowing on his chilblained fingers and grinned.

'It's you, chapman. Hob and I've wondered how you were doing, if you were up and about yet. A nasty turn you had there. But Mistress Walker will've looked after you. A good woman, that, whatever some people might whisper behind her back. But then, some'd whisper about their own grandmothers. You're still seemingly a bit pale, though. Get plenty of her good victuals inside you. Now what can I do for you?'

I explained as best I could without taking up too much of his time, for I could see his partner was waiting to hang a new length of cloth which had just been brought from the fulling yard. 'I understand it was your two lads,' I ended, 'who fished William Woodward's hat from the River Frome. Alderman Weaver suggested I speak to them if I could find them.'

Burl scratched his head thoughtfully. 'They might be at home with their mother this time o' day, but mostly they're out getting into mischief. A pair o' rascals, and always have been. But the elder, Jack, 'll soon be starting his apprenticeship, praise be to St Katherine, for he's to be a weaver, unlike me. This job's not fit for a dog in winter. He's to go to Master Adelard in Redcliffe Hill. As to this other business of William Woodward, speak to them by all means, though I doubt either Jack or Dick'll be able to tell you more'n they've told already. All the same, I'd be glad to have the mystery cleared if it were possible. It's been hard on those two women.'

'Where do you live?' I asked, as he turned away to grasp his end of the wet cloth which the second man was pulling from the basket.

'Hard by Temple Church, near the rope-walk. Knock on any door. Anyone'll tell you where me and my Jenny live.'

I left him and his partner struggling with the weight of the red-dyed cloth, fixing it between the two sets of tenterhooks, and retraced my footsteps back through the Redcliffe Gate. I followed the line of the city walls to my right and came eventually to the rope-walk, where two men, one at either end of the stretch of gravel, were twisting strands of hempen fibre into an inch-thick rope. Temple Church stood on the corner of Temple Street and Water Lane, and I was quickly directed to Burl Hodge's cottage, where the door was answered by a young, fresh-faced woman in a brown homespun woollen gown. In spite of being flushed from the exertions of cooking, for she was obviously preparing the midday meal, she gave me a smile as wide as her husband's and invited me inside.

For the second time that morning I repeated my story, while Jenny Hodge brought me a cup of small ale and two of her oatcakes to sample. When I had finished, she said: 'You're in luck. The boys have gone to fetch my bread from the baker's oven, and they should be back any minute. Thursday,' she added, 'is Water Lane's day for baking.'

Even as she spoke, the door opened and two young lads came in, carrying a large, covered basket. The scent of newly baked bread filled the room, and it was hardly surprising that, ignoring my presence, Jack and Dick Hodge immediately clamoured for a slice off one of the loaves.

'In a minute,' their mother replied sternly, 'when you've spoken to this gentleman. Listen to what he has to say and answer him nicely.'

Two round, freckled faces, small counterparts of their father's, were turned towards me with an inquiring air, and the boys flopped down on the bench beside me. I repeated my request for a third time.

Jack explored his nose with a probing finger while considering his answer. 'It was just a hat,' he said at last, 'wasn't it, Dick? Except there were bloodstains on it.'

'Bloodstains,' his brother echoed with ghoulish satisfaction.

Jack continued, 'We don't usually fish the Frome. Mother doesn't like us going across the city, so we stay beside the Avon. But that day, well, we thought we'd like a change, didn't we, Dick?'

'Like a change,' Dick assured me dutifully.

'Did you catch anything?' I asked, diverted. 'Apart from the hat, I mean.'

71

Two heads nodded in unison. 'A cod, that long.' Jack held up his hands to indicate a length of well over two feet, while his brother went one better and spread wide his arms. 'And then we found the hat. It caught on the end of my line.'

'End of his line,' Dick said, smiling.

'What sort of hat?' I returned Dick's smile.

Jack shrugged, a gesture at once copied by his brother. I wondered how the younger boy would fare when the elder went to live with Master Adelard, the weaver.

'Just a plain hat,' Jack said, 'with a wide brim. All soggy it was, but you could see darker patches on it. We didn't know it was dried blood then,' he admitted reluctantly.

'But you knew who it belonged to?'

'We guessed. We'd all heard about Master Woodward being missing.'

'So what did you do with it?'

'We meant to take it to Mistress Walker, but Master Herepath just happened along at that moment, so we gave it to him.'

'Master Edward Herepath?'

Jack opened his eyes wide at my stupidity. 'Of course. His brother was in the Newgate prison.'

'Newgate prison,' came the expected echo.

I interrogated them for a few moments longer, but it soon became apparent that they had no more to tell. They could recall nothing other than what they told the sheriff's officers at the time; and even those few details were fading from their minds. Each new day presented them with ever-expanding horizons, and the events of almost a twelve-month since held no interest for them. I thanked them both with solemn courtesy and rose to take my leave. Released from the need to be polite, the boys whooped around their mother, clamouring for a slice of bread, preferably one of the golden-baked crusts.

Fending them off with practised hands, Jenny Hodge escorted me to the door just as someone knocked. A man stood outside, muffled in his cloak against the cold, its hood pulled well forward to conceal his face. Nevertheless, Jenny had no difficulty in identifying her visitor and gave a nervous start.

'Oh!' she said, 'it's you.' She glanced sideways at me, then held the door wide. 'Burl's from home at present, but he'll be back soon for his dinner. You'd . . . You'd best come in and wait.'

'Thank you, Mistress.' The man stepped across the threshold without sparing me a look, keeping his head lowered so that the hood fell even further forward about his face. He said nothing else before Jenny Hodge ushered me out and closed the door behind me, yet somehow I felt as though I had heard that voice before, and recently. I racked my brains, repeating the unknown's words over and over inside my head, but gradually I lost the intonation and gave up trying to remember. I told myself that I was probably mistaken.

I returned to Alderman Weaver's counting-house, to find him pacing up and down. The aulnager had been gone a little while, all the alderman's cloth being of the required width, with no thin patches from the use of inferior wool. Each roll now bore the aulnager's seal, and awaited collection by the carter.

'Ah, there you are at last,' was the impatient greeting. 'Here's the letter you wanted for Master Herepath.' The alderman held out a thin sheet of parchment, then snatched it back again. 'He has suffered greatly. You must promise me not to hound him should he refuse to see you.'

I gave my word willingly, for if God did not mean me to solve this mystery, then I could be on the road once more. And without the assistance of the hanged man's brother, I doubted that I should learn very much. I said my farewells and thanked the alderman for his help. My stomach was telling me that it was time for dinner, a sure sign I was getting better, and I turned my feet in the direction of Margaret Walker's cottage.

It was as I made my way along St Thomas's Street that I recalled where, and in what circumstances, I had heard the voice of Jenny Hodge's visitor before. Until that moment, I would have deemed it impossible that it was one and the same, for the voice of Margaret Walker's nocturnal caller during my illness had been muted; nothing more, I would have sworn, than an indistinguishable murmur to my straining ears. Now, however, I realized it must have sounded plainer than I thought, for I knew beyond doubt that on both occasions, the speaker had been the same man.

Chapter Seven

There was leek pottage for dinner, heavily laced with garlic to disguise the lack of other flavours at this dead time of the year; but, eaten with thick slabs of oatmeal bread, it warmed and filled the belly. In addition, there was ale for me and verjuice for the women, made from last autumn's harvest of crab-apples. While we ate, I recounted the history of my morning, but said nothing of the Hodges' visitor, nor of my suspicions concerning him. Instinct told me that I should learn no more if I did. I should be treated to vacant stares and a flat denial of any such caller at the cottage. And I had been ill enough at the time for the incident to be attributed to my delirious fancy.

I did, however, ask Margaret Walker about her father's return, and to all my questions she answered with apparent frankness.

'His boots were thick with dust,' she said, 'as though he had been walking for days on the road. But as for getting any sense out of him as to where he had been, I told you before, that was well-nigh impossible. All he would say, when he was able to say anything, was that he had been captured by slavers and taken to Ireland. Never a word would he vouchsafe about what part of Ireland, how he had escaped from bondage, what ship had brought him home.' She shrugged and gave a sad, wry smile. 'But of course he couldn't. He was never in Ireland. For that's the conclusion we were all forced to in the end.'

I nodded. 'So Alderman Weaver believes, and confirmed your opinion that no one would have wanted to buy an old and injured man. Slavers, he maintained, would not have beaten a captive about the head in such a brutal fashion as to cause him to lose his wits.'

Lillis, who had eaten very little, being too busy watching me with her slanting eyes, asked softly, 'Then where was he? And why should he believe he had been taken to Ireland?'

Margaret put in swiftly, to save me the embarrassment of doubting her father's word, 'Perhaps he didn't. Perhaps he knew where he had been and why, but for reasons of his own did not wish anyone else to know. Although,' she added, encountering her daughter's derisive smile, 'I am inclined to the view that he really remembered very little of anything that had happened to him. Even events prior to his disappearance were hazy in his mind, and it was necessary to go back many years before he was able to recall things with any clarity. He knew that he had lived with Lillis and me, in this cottage, which was why he returned here and not to his home in Bell Lane, but that was four years and more ago.'

I finished my stew and laid down my spoon, resisting Margaret's attempts to ladle me out a second helping. I drank my ale, conscious of a sudden thirst, before asking, 'And there's nothing else you can tell me which might shed any light on where Master Woodward had been?'

I knew by her expression that something had puzzled her. She sucked her teeth thoughtfully, clearing them of bits of food, staring straight ahead but seeing nothing. I waited patiently, content to let her take her time.

'It was his clothes,' she said at last. Her eyes swivelled round to meet mine. 'They weren't his. They weren't any that I'd ever seen before.'

'Someone had robbed him of his, perhaps,' I suggested, when she paused. 'Or his had been torn and bloodied so badly when he was captured that he had to be found new ones to wear. There are probably half a dozen reasons.'

She nodded slowly. 'Maybe, but these were good clothes. Rich clothes. The hose were pure wool, the doublet velvet, the shirt and drawers of fine, bleached linen. Gentleman's garments, every one. The boots, although well-worn and rubbed, were made of Spanish leather, and there was also a hooded cape, lined with silk and scalloped round the edges.'

'Don't forget the cloak,' Lillis reminded her mother.

'Oh yes, the cloak.' Abstractedly, Margaret Walker stirred the remains of her soup around the bottom of her wooden bowl. 'It's true it was made of frieze, but it was fur-lined, and none of your sheepskin or badger or cat! It was squirrel, a delicate grey colour and beautifully soft.'

77

I was intrigued. 'What happened to them when your father died?'

'I still have them. They were too good to part with and I folded them in lavender and put them away in the chest.' She nodded towards the stout oaken coffer ranged against one wall. 'I'll show you them if you'd like.'

She rose, selecting one of the keys from the bunch which hung at her belt, inserted it in the chest's iron lock, and lifted the lid. The room was immediately filled with the sweet intermingled scents of musk and violet and lavender. Having removed her own and Lillis's best gowns from the top, she stooped and brought out, almost reverently, the pile of clothes beneath.

I went to stand beside her. We once more closed the lid of the chest and placed them on top. Gently I picked up each garment, shook it out, and held it up to the light filtering through the parchment of the window. The velvet doublet was a dull amber colour, very rich, but lacking the tightly nipped waist which had become so fashionable among the wealthy in recent years. The drawers and shirt, as Margaret had said, were of fine, bleached linen, the hood and cape lined with scarlet cendal. And the frieze cloak was indeed lined with the soft grey fur of squirrel. The apparel of a gentleman, and one more reason, if another was needed, to doubt that William Woodward had come by them as a slave in Ireland. But there was nothing else, alas, to suggest where they might have come from, or how William had obtained them. I did notice one thing, however, on closer examination. The seams of the garments were strained and in some places beginning to part. The boots, also, showed the imprint of feet slightly too large for them. The soft Spanish leather had been pushed out of shape at the base of each big toe, and the toes themselves had bulged in protest against their too rigid confinement. A well-built man had owned these boots and clothes, but not so well-built as William Woodward.

Beyond that, however, they told me nothing, and I helped Margaret return them to the chest, covering them again with the two women's gowns. There were other things in the chest; I noticed sheets, neatly folded, and a woollen blanket such as the one I used at nights, a pair of old shoes, some spare hose and a cloak of that thick, coarse material we used to call burel. There was also the edge of what looked like a book: I had a fleeting glimpse of rubbed velvet binding and the protruding edges of vellum. But before I could be sure of what I had seen, Margaret had replaced the clothes, slammed the lid of the chest and locked it. Had I been mistaken?

I asked, and Margaret Walker laughed, but to my ears there was something forced about the sound. 'What would poor people, who can neither read nor write, be doing with books?' she mocked. 'Why would they spend good money on something that would be of no use to them?'

Lillis, who was heating water over the fire in order to wash the dishes, said nothing. A small, contemptuous smile tilted the corners of her mouth, but whether the object of her disdain was myself or her mother, I had no means of knowing. And the more I thought about what I had seen, the less able I was to picture it clearly. As Margaret had pointed out, a book or folio would be an unlikely item to find in such a dwelling. I noted, however, that she did not offer to unlock the chest and solve the mystery. So my suspicions remained, but I had no means of verifying either their truth or falsity.

'What will you do now?' Lillis asked me.

I put my hand inside my leather pouch and produced the letter. 'Alderman Weaver has kindly provided me with the means of introduction to Edward Herepath. I shall visit him this afternoon and hope to find him at home. If not, I shall return tomorrow.'

Both women were obviously impressed by the fact that my boast to know the alderman had been no idle one. At the same time, I again sensed that uneasiness in Margaret Walker as though, much as she wished to discover the truth behind her father's disappearance, she nevertheless was frightened by what I might uncover. She made no demur, however, at my plans, beyond remarking that Nick Brimble was bringing his truckle bed for me sometime today, and might have been glad of a helping hand.

'Tell me where he lives, and I'll fetch it myself this evening,' I offered promptly.

She shook her head. 'Lillis can aid Nick after she returns from the dyer's with the new batch of wool. And hurry up with those pots, girl!' she scolded. 'I need the room to get on with my spinning.'

Lillis's face darkened angrily, and I could foresee one of those furious spats which enlivened the existence of mother and daughter, but which were so distressing to outsiders. Cravenly I made my escape, thankfully latching the door behind me as, warmly wrapped in my good frieze cloak, I stepped into the street.

In spite of my letter from Alderman Weaver, I knew better than to knock on Edward Herepath's front door, if there were any other entrance. Having ascertained which house was his, I walked the length of Small Street and turned into Bell Lane, where William Woodward had lived. I looked curiously at the two rows of dwellings, one on either side of the roadway, but had no time just then for more than a cursory glance, as I had found what I was seeking. A narrow alleyway, such as served the houses of neighbouring Broad Street, also ran along the back of those in Small Street. High walls enclosed each plot of ground, with stout oaken, iron-studded gates giving access to the gardens.

At the third one, I stopped and tried the latch. It wasn't bolted. I opened the gate and stepped into a garden similar to that of Alderman Weaver. An apple tree raised naked and twisted branches towards the overcast sky, and nothing showed above the hard, brown earth which still bore traces of the morning's frost. In summer, it would be full of flowers and sweet fragrance; now all was as black and dead as the time of year.

Immediately to my left, just inside the gate, was a small stone outbuilding, two of its four sides being the garden walls which separated Edward Herepath's property from the lane and that of his neighbour. The sloping roof was made of good lead tiles and the door, again of stout, iron-studded oak, was set in the short wall which faced me. I glanced towards the house, but the back windows were shuttered to keep out the cold and no one had, as yet, espied me. Cautiously, I tried the door of the outbuilding which, in spite of its keyhole, and greatly to my surprise, I found to be unlocked. Feeling like a thief, I stepped inside.

Within, it was dank and cheerless, the only source of light coming from the open doorway. A few garden tools were ranged along one wall, and there was a shelf holding candlestick, flint and tinder, together with a pestle and mortar. A stool stood in one corner, and there were some withered plant stems on the beaten-earth floor. I emerged once more into the garden.

My knock on what I supposed was the kitchen door produced no immediate response, but a second, louder rap brought the sound of a woman's voice, soft but speaking with authority. 'It's all right, Mistress Hardacre, I will see who it is. There is no need to trouble yourself. The sauce will curdle if you don't keep stirring.'

The door opened and a young woman stood on the threshold. An almost perfect oval face, with the creamiest, smoothest skin and bluest eyes that I have ever seen, stared back at me, the fair brows lifted in inquiry. She wore a blue woollen dress with long loose sleeves, tied at the waist with an embroidered girdle. Her hair, the colour of ripe corn and coiled around the shapely head in two thick plaits, was just visible beneath a white gauze veil. I have seen many women in my life, both before and since, far more beautiful than Cicely Ford, but never one who exuded such goodness and inner beauty. There was a strength and serenity about her which made me long to lay my head on her breast and unburden all my troubles.

'I . . . I have a letter for M-Master Herepath,' I stuttered, before pulling myself together. 'From his friend, Alderman Weaver.' I took it out of my pouch and handed it to her. 'If you would be so gracious as to take it to him and ask him to read it . . .' My voice tailed away like that of any green and tongue-tied boy.

'Please come in.' She sounded as sweet as she looked, and I found myself blushing stupidly as I stepped inside the kitchen. A round, plump robin of a woman in a black dress and white hood was stirring the contents of a pan hanging from a hook over the fire. She glanced up, smiling vaguely in my direction, but her task absorbed all her attention and she quickly returned to it with anxious eyes. If she were the housekeeper, as I supposed she must be, she seemed the very opposite of the dragon who ruled the alderman's household. But I was no more interested in her than she was in me: I was conscious only of an overriding impatience to see and speak to Cicely Ford again.

I realized suddenly that she had not told me her name, but who else could she be? She exactly fitted Margaret Walker's description of her, and such a woman would naturally excite Lillis's derision. One was as fair as the other

was dark, as open and sweet-natured as the other was sly
and secretive. It was ridiculous! I had known Cicely Ford
for only a few moments, exchanged less than three dozen
words with her, but I was falling in love.

She returned presently, a slight frown creasing her
brow. She regarded me warily, hostility being foreign to
her nature, but it was plain that I was not as welcome as
I had been.

'Master Herepath will see you,' she said. 'Please
follow me.'

She led me out of the kitchen, past the buttery and
across the hall to the parlour. The hall was a fine room,
hung with tapestries of hunting scenes in rich reds and
greens and blues. A fire burned on the big, open hearth
beneath the intricately carved stone mantel, which was
also picked out in shades of red and blue; and at either
end of the long trestle table which occupied the middle
of the floor stood two handsomely carved armchairs. The
parlour was smaller and snugger, and a second fire burned
on a hearth which shared the wide chimney of the hall.
A third armchair was pulled close to the warmth, a broad
window-seat was strewn with green velvet cushions, a
five-branched candlestick of latten tin stood atop a spruce
coffer with delicate scrollwork round the lid and, luxury
of luxuries, rugs, not rushes, were scattered over the floor.
Edward Herepath was obviously a very wealthy man.

As we entered, he rose to his feet, but I was not foolish
enough to imagine that either the courtesy or the smile
of welcome were for me. He held out his hand and drew

his ward to him. 'Why don't you find Dame Freda?' he asked gently. 'She was complaining only this morning that your embroidery is still unfinished.'

Cicely Ford shook her head decisively. She was a young woman who knew her own mind and quietly, but determinedly, got her own way. 'If this conversation is to be about Robert, then I wish to stay.'

'It will only upset you, sweetheart. Go, to please me.'

The sweet mouth set in stubborn lines and she once again shook her head. Tears brimmed in the cornflower-blue eyes. 'And why should I not be upset?' Her voice was bitter. 'What have I done that I should be spared his memory more than you? Did I remain loyal when he needed me most? Did I believe him any more than the jury when he swore he was innocent of murder? Did I heed his plea to me from prison to go to see him one last time? No!' The cry was that of a mortally wounded animal and pierced me to the heart. She buried her face in her hands, sobbing in great distress.

I realized, as I had often done in the past, that uncovering the truth is a painful process and sometimes can do more harm than good. I was half inclined to turn tail there and then, to return to Mistress Walker and tell her that to pursue the quest would bring unnecessary suffering to one of the sweetest girls I had ever met. My mouth was even open to take my leave, but somehow the words would not come. Some instinct held me silent, and it was not just an unwillingness to face Lillis's mocking smile, nor simply my overwhelming curiosity in these matters.

I was seized once more, as had happened to me twice before, by the conviction that evil was at work and had to be destroyed, or God would never let me rest.

Accepting defeat, Edward Herepath turned his attention to me. Cicely Ford retired to the window-seat, averting her face until she had her features once more under control.

Her guardian resumed his seat by the fire and looked up, unsmiling. 'Well, Master Chapman, you see what a hornet's nest you are stirring up about our ears. But I owe it to my good friend Alderman Weaver at least to hear what you have to say.'

Chapter Eight

Edward Herepath was a handsome man, tall, broad-shouldered, with a heavily jowled face and a square chin made even more so by a short, square-cut beard. Both beard and hair, the latter modishly cropped just below the ears, were dark brown, shot through with glints of red, and the eyes were that indeterminate shade of blue which in certain lights can easily be mistaken for grey. His tunic of russet-coloured wool was not so short as might have been worn by a younger man – the male fashion in those days was for an almost vulgar emphasis on loins and buttocks – but neither was it so long as to risk being dubbed outdated. His shoes, of fine green leather, were fashionably piked, but again reasonably so, the pointed toes still allowing ease of movement. Altogether, I decided, a man who took pride in his appearance, but also one conscious of his dignity and not prepared to sacrifice it by succumbing to the extreme follies of youth.

'Well?' he prompted, after a moment of tongue-tied silence on my part. 'You wish to talk to me about my brother. You are lodging, so Alderman Weaver informs me, with Mistress Walker and her daughter, Lillis.'

'Yes. I was taken ill some weeks ago, on my arrival in Bristol, and these women were good enough to take me in and nurse me back to health. In due time they told me their story. It distresses them that people look at them askance, as though they were privy to whatever happened to Master Woodward. I have therefore promised that, insofar as it is possible, I will try to discover the truth.'

Edward Herepath raised strongly marked eyebrows. 'And you desire my blessing?' His voice grew harsh. 'What is done is done, and nothing you or anyone can find out now will give my brother back his life. It is a tragedy which Mistress Ford and I must learn to live with, but at least time may reconcile us in some small degree to the dreadful consequences. If, however, you rake over the dead ashes of our grief, then you risk inflaming them anew.'

Before I could make reply, Cicely Ford slid off the window-seat and came forward to stand behind her guardian's chair, one delicate, blue-veined hand pressing his shoulder.

'Edward,' she said quietly, 'I understand how you feel. Indeed, who better? But the truth can harm no one. Perhaps we ourselves would benefit from knowing exactly what happened. And we cannot let the innocent suffer unjustly. If, as Master Chapman says, Mistress Walker and her daughter are being held responsible for Master Woodward's actions by some members of the weavers' brotherhood, then that is unfair, for I would stake my life that they knew no more than he did, poor man. I only wish you had felt able to visit him with me, for you would have seen for yourself that he had been so greatly abused that he retained no knowledge of what had befallen him. And the women were equally bewildered.'

Edward Herepath raised one of his hands and covered hers, but did not speak for several moments. It was plain to me that he was in a dilemma. His natural instinct was to let sleeping dogs lie, or, as he himself had put it, not to rake over old ashes. At the same time he wanted to please Cicely. If she had the courage to face renewed suffering in order to alleviate that of other people, then he had no wish to appear a coward in her eyes. To refuse my request would make him seem callous, indifferent to Margaret Walker's situation.

He twisted round and looked at her. 'Sweetheart, are you sure of this? Is it what you really want? Consider! Just by coming here this afternoon, Master Chapman has already caused us both great pain, and will probably grieve us more before he has finished. And for what? There is no certainty that he will be able to discover any-thing. Indeed, I consider it highly unlikely. I made what inquiries I could at the time, as did Alderman Weaver on behalf of Mistress Walker and her daughter. But to no avail.' He gently squeezed Cicely's hand. 'Will you not be guided by me, and let the matter rest?'

Cicely stooped, kissing him lightly on the forehead, and as she did so, I noticed how convulsively his other hand gripped his chair arm. It came to me that Edward Herepath, too, had fallen under the spell of this lovely girl; that he felt more for her than just the protective affection of a guardian. My heart went out to him, for it was not simply that he was so much older than she, nor that the love she felt for him was so obviously filial, but that even if he were able, eventually, to overcome both these obstacles, he could never hope to rival a dead man. And not just a dead man, but one who commanded Cicely's eternal devotion and penance. For whatever Robert Herepath's shortcomings in life, however much misery he had caused, the nature and circumstances of his death ensured him the status of a martyr in her eyes. Her fragile shoulders were bowed down by a weight of guilt almost too great for her to bear. And against all that, how could Edward Herepath possibly compete?

Cicely came round the side of his chair and knelt down, looking up at him earnestly. 'Dear Edward, I do understand your misgivings, but please let me have my way in this. I feel a great need to find out as much as I can about the reasons for Robert's death. There is so much unexplained, not least the sense that some evil was abroad which set every man's hand against him. Oh, I know what you would say! That Robert himself was the cause, but I refuse to accept that. In part it was true. He was wild, he didn't care who he offended. But that doesn't explain why we all turned on him and believed him guilty of murder, even though there was no body. You and Alderman Weaver have done your best to discover the truth, and failed. So give this young man a chance. The alderman speaks of him in his letter as the person responsible for finding out what happened to his son. If that is so, then maybe he can unravel this mystery for us.' She gripped Edward's sleeve until her knuckles showed white against the russet. 'Please. For my sake, give him leave to try.'

I don't know who could have resisted her pleading, the blinding tears in those cornflower-blue eyes. Certainly I could not, and neither it appeared could Edward Herepath, for he heaved a resigned sigh and patted her cheek. 'Dry your eyes, my dear child. If it means so much to you, I'll grant the chapman my blessing, albeit reluctantly.'

Cicely gave him a watery smile and rose to her feet, dabbing her eyes with a fragment of embroidered linen. It was the first time I had ever seen anyone use a handkerchief, although they had been a commonplace among the nobility since their introduction almost a hundred years before by King Richard. I had a sudden, vivid picture of how Lillis would look if she cried, red-nosed and sniffing loudly, and could not help contrasting it with the restrained emotion of the girl in front of me. Cicely Ford had completely bewitched me.

Edward Herepath straightened his back, placed the tips of his fingers together and regarded me straitly. 'Very well, young man, as Mistress Ford is so insistent you should try, you have my permission to inquire into Master Woodward's disappearance and find out what you can. Is there anything you would wish to ask me?'

Cicely retired once more to the window-seat, out of my

line of vision, and I regretfully tore my eyes away to re-focus them on her guardian.

'I was wondering, sir, if you could explain how it was that William Woodward came to work for you as your debt collector when he had spent all his life in weaving and, moreover, at an age when his daughter thought him too old to work much longer.'

Edward Herepath frowned. 'Is such questioning strictly necessary? Very well! Very well! I gave my word.' This at a slight stirring behind him from Cicely. He continued testily, 'I cannot recollect all the circumstances. It is almost five years ago. He had never been more than an indifferent weaver. His masterpiece was never accepted by the Guild and he remained a journeyman all his life. The man I employed to collect my rents had recently married a Keynsham girl and had quit my service to live in her home village. He had given me very little prior warning and I needed someone quickly to take his place.'

'But why William Woodward?' I persisted.

Edward shrugged irritably. 'I believe, if memory serves me aright, that he asked himself if he might enter my employ. He was tired of living with his daughter. There were disagreements between them, and he knew that the cottage in Bell Lane was my property and always let, rent free, to my debt collector. He fancied his independence and considered himself capable of doing the job.'

'But did *you*?' I persisted. 'William Woodward was not a young man. According to Mistress Walker's calculations, her father must have been in his fifty-ninth year when he abandoned weaving and came to work for you. An advanced age for a man to be still working at the looms, let alone taking up the strenuous task of debt collecting. Did none of these things weigh with you?'

Edward Herepath frowned and stirred angrily in his chair. I realized that my questioning had been too blunt and, as well, had probably sounded a note of censure which he rightly resented. He had allowed me to interrogate him as a favour. I must watch my step.

Nevertheless, he answered with only a hint of testiness. 'William Woodward was a big, strong man, well set-up, for all that he was grey-haired. People were a little afraid of him, a little in awe of his size and strength. At least, that was my impression. Yes, I did think him capable of doing the job, and doing it well, and my belief was justified. During the four years he was in my employ, I had fewer bad debts than theretofore. As you may have been told, I have much property both in and around Bristol, and William was adept at making certain the rents were collected. I did not inquire what methods he used to ensure prompt payment. I was merely thankful that the unpleasantness of calling on the sheriff's officers to evict or threaten defaulters became less and less frequent.' Once again, Edward Herepath frowned, but this time it was not I who was the object of his disapproval. 'Perhaps I was wrong not to keep a stricter eye on William. Maybe he made greater enemies than Miles Huckbody, who, I know, swore vengeance on him on more than one occasion.'

'Miles Huckbody?' I queried.

Edward Herepath roused himself from a momentary reverie and, reaching out with one elegantly shod foot, kicked the slumbering fire into life. Flames licked at the edges of the logs, sending shadows soaring. The blues and ochres of the wall-hangings faded, and the reds ran together, mingling like blood.

'What? Oh, Miles Huckbody. His wife and child rented a cottage and field from me near the King's Wood, but the man fell ill and was unable to work the land. His wife struggled as best she could for a while, but the crops dwindled and the pig died and they were eventually unable to produce enough to live on, let alone to sell.' Edward Herepath sighed. 'Instead of consulting me, William took it upon himself to have the family evicted and, by the time I was aware of what had happened, it was too late. They had gone. But Miles Huckbody later reappeared in Bristol. His wife and child had apparently died, and he himself was sick and destitute. He was taken in by the fraternity of the Bons-Hommes, who run the Gaunts' Hospital close by Saint Augustine's Abbey. They clothe, feed and house some hundred poor souls, thanks to the charitable munificence, two centuries or more ago, of Maurice and Henry de Gaunt and their nephew, Robert de Gourney.' He added with civic pride: 'Bristol folk look after their own.'

But not enough, I thought, to prevent their eviction in the first place. On the other hand, business is business, as any Bristolian, then or now, will tell you.

Aloud, I asked, 'And Miles Huckbody is known to have threatened the well-being of Master Woodward?'

'So William himself informed me. He met the man once, down in the broad meads, near the house of the Dominican friars, and was roundly abused by Huckbody, who offered him violence, and was only just restrained by fellow inmates from the hospital. Not that William thought himself in any danger. Miles Huckbody was too feeble, he said, to pose any threat or cause him any loss of sleep.'

'All the same,' I said, 'William Woodward had at least one known enemy who wished him harm.'

Edward Herepath shrugged. 'More than one I should imagine. He was not a man who endeared himself to people. Blunt, taciturn, and bearing a grudge against the world for the way he felt life had cheated him, is how I would sum up William Woodward. Yet I got on with him well enough, perhaps because I, too, had had my cross to bear.'

He spoke with quiet bitterness, and without stopping to recollect Cicely Ford's presence in the room. Only when she cried out, a sound suppressed almost as soon as it was uttered, did he remember and rise hurriedly to his feet, hands outstretched. 'My dear child! I did not mean . . . Forgive me! You know I would not willingly add to your grief.'

Cicely dropped her embroidery and grasped both his hands in hers. 'No, no! There is nothing to forgive. I know how much you had to bear from Robert, how disorderly and disobedient he could be. I know, also, how much he had to be grateful to you for; how you looked after and watched over him all his life from the time he was two years old. No one could have had a kinder, more forbearing brother. He realized it, too, though he could never be prevailed upon to acknowledge it openly. But you and I, dear Edward, both know that under all that wildness, he was good and kind; that there was a real sweetness of nature which would have surfaced after his marriage to me. I could have tamed him. I know I could!'

Edward Herepath returned the pressure of her hands, his eyes looking steadfastly into hers. 'Who could doubt it? Your gentleness and beauty are such that they must prevail with any man in time.'

He stooped and kissed one of the hands he was holding, before guiltily dropping both and turning away, an expression of defeated longing on his face. I felt desperately sorry for him, understanding all that he must be suffering, for Cicely Ford was weaving her own brand of magic about me, filling my mind with a strange yearning, conjuring up fantasies of things which could never be.

Edward Herepath resumed his seat beside the fire and glanced up at me. My legs were beginning to ache with inactivity, for he had not offered me a stool. 'Is there anything else you wish to ask?' he inquired.

I hesitated, sensing that his patience was wearing thin, but reluctant to take my leave before I had satisfied my curiosity still further. At last, I ventured, 'You were in Gloucester when the seeming murder of William Woodward occurred.'

'Indeed. I had gone to look over a horse with a view to purchase. An acquaintance of my friend Master Peter Avenel had told me of his intent to sell whilst staying in Bristol a few weeks earlier. The animal sounded exactly suited to my requirements, and I therefore made arrangements to travel north as soon as possible after Master Shottery's return to his native city. I rode to Gloucester on Lady Day and took lodgings for two nights at an inn. This gave me the morrow to look over the horse and make up my mind whether or not to buy, and a third day in which to return home at my leisure, which is exactly how things fell out.' A look of distress contorted his handsome features. 'As it happened, I could well have returned a day earlier, for the purchase was speedily concluded early on the Friday morning, but Master Shottery was unable to offer me hospitality, as his wife, he said, was feeling unwell. However, I decided to adhere to my original plan and remain in Gloucester until the following day.'

Cicely said quietly from the window-seat behind him, 'You must not blame yourself, dear Edward. Your earlier return would have prevented nothing. Little though any of us knew it at the time, the mischief, whatever it was, was already done.'

I asked abruptly: 'You were not anxious, Master Herepath, as to what might have happened in your absence, knowing that you had, at least according to Mistress Walker, inadvertently let slip to your brother that William Woodward was holding the money until you came home?'

Edward Herepath's face flushed a dull red beneath its beard. I held my breath, waiting to be dismissed for my impudence, but instead provoking a small, if wintry, smile. 'You take your commission seriously, Master Chapman. Mistress Walker and her daughter appear to have chosen their champion wisely. Very well, yes, I admit to having felt a twinge of uneasiness every now and then. But my brother had been the cause of so much worry throughout his life that I had grown accustomed to such feelings, as one might grow used to the nagging pain of an old wound which, with time, one is able to ignore. Does that answer satisfy you? I trust so, for it's the only excuse I have.'

I gave a little bow. 'You have been more than gracious, Master Herepath, and I thank you for bearing so patiently with my questions. With your permission, I shall now take my leave.'

He rose to his feet once more, good humour restored at the prospect of my departure. And who could blame him? My probing must have awakened many painful memories which he was trying to forget.

'Both Mistress Ford and I hope that we have been of some service to you. Have you any idea, as yet, what could possibly have happened to William Woodward?'

I shook my head. 'I confess to being as much in the dark as ever, but I shall certainly seek out this Miles Huckbody and question him. Mistress Ford, your humble servant. And yours, sir. Thank you, and God be with you. If it is not too presumptuous, I shall keep you both in my prayers.'

Chapter Nine

Cicely Ford rose immediately from her place by the window and accompanied me to the door. I noted the slight frown of disapproval on Edward Herepath's face and guessed that her willingness to serve others irritated him. He wanted to revere her, isolate her from the common herd, set her apart from the mundane rigours of everyday life, but that was plainly not her way. Without displaying any trace of humility, Cicely Ford was happy to be of use, and refused to leave everything to servants in a house where, I suspected, young as she was, she had been virtual mistress since the death of her guardian's wife some three years previously.

As the door to the parlour shut behind us, she laid a detaining hand on my arm, urging me closer to the fire burning on the hall hearth, and out of the draught whistling in from the buttery, which lifted the rushes on the floor. 'Warm yourself properly before you go out again,' she said. 'The streets today are bitter.'

Nothing loath, for every delay was an added moment

in her company, I held out my hands to the blaze. After a minute or two, presuming on her natural friendliness and summoning up my courage, I asked gently, 'Would you indeed have married Robert Herepath, had he lived?'

The blue eyes opened wide, once again full of tears, and I glimpsed such anguish in their swimming depths that it was like a descent into hell. I averted my own gaze swiftly, uncomfortably aware that I had trespassed on private ground; seen what I should not have seen. Before I could apologize, however, she whispered, 'Yes.'

A log crackled, sending up a shower of sparks. 'Forgive me . . .' I was beginning, but she did not hear me, wrapped as she was in her overwhelming grief. Then, suddenly, she spoke, the words bursting forth in a torrent from her overcharged heart. 'Do you know what it is like to fail the one person you love more than life itself in his hour of need? To believe him capable of the heinous crime of murder? To allow yourself to feel a revulsion so great that you turn from him in horror? Do you?' She twisted her hands together so tightly that it seemed the delicate fingers must crack, but she was unconscious of the pain. 'No, of course you don't! And I pray to God in His mercy that you never will!' She drew in her breath sharply, rearing her head on its slender neck. 'I loved Robert Herepath from the moment I first became aware of him, when I was still a child, long before my father died and left me in Edward's care. I knew that whatever he appeared to be, however spoiled and reckless and ungrateful, he was not really like that underneath. He was a man who had never grown up. He needed gentleness and affection and understanding. Oh, Edward loved him as much as I did in his own way. But he was always busy and had too little time to spare for a younger brother left in his care.' She lifted sad eyes to mine. 'Please don't think I'm blaming Edward. He was not much more than twenty when Giles Herepath died and he found himself father and mother both to a boy of barely two.' A shy smile curled her lips. 'That was the year I was born, but my own father often spoke to me of the burden Edward had so willingly shouldered, and how much he admired him for it.'

I thought that her unreasoning love for Robert Herepath had blinded her to a character ruined by an over-indulgent brother, and vitiated even further by a naturally vicious streak. I kept my views to myself, but ventured to ask, 'Why then were you as certain as everyone else that Robert had murdered William Woodward? Especially as no body was found, only William's hat which had been flung into the Frome.'

Cicely Ford shivered, in spite of the heat from the fire, and clasped her arms about her body as though she would never be warm again. 'I don't know! *I don't know.* Looking back now, it all seems like an evil dream.' She furrowed her brow, as though trying to make sense of the nightmare. 'Perhaps . . . Perhaps it was because Edward was so sure his brother had done it. Edward is not a man to be easily deceived, yet he told me himself that he was convinced of Robert's guilt as soon as he was in possession of the facts. He blamed himself bitterly for having put temptation in Robert's path, but the absence of William Woodward's body in no way disposed him to believe his brother's protestations of innocence. His conviction somehow influenced me and blinded me to the truth.'

'Robert admitted to stealing the money?' I asked, seeking confirmation of Mistress Walker's story.

'Oh, yes. He was always truthful, about his vices as well as his virtues.' Again, the fingers writhed together in anguish. 'I knew it, and that fact alone should have assured me of his innocence of the greater crime. Yet still I let myself be persuaded of his guilt.'

There was a splutter among the logs, and a small, blue flame spurted up the chimney. 'You were willing to forgive him so much,' I suggested tentatively. 'Could you not forgive him murder as well?'

The cornflower-blue eyes raised to mine were filled with abhorrence. 'The taking of human life for gain? No, that I could never condone.' Her voice fell almost to a whisper. 'That men must be killed, in war, by the law: that I accept; but otherwise, the right is God's and God's alone!'

I might have pressed the matter further, arguing that in this case the law had obviously been mistaken, but at that moment there was a knock on the street door, and a woman appeared on the half-landing of the staircase which ascended from the hall to the upper storeys of the house. 'That will surely be Master Robin,' she said in a tone of deep satisfaction.

She descended the remaining stairs, an upright, sprightly woman of some forty summers, dressed all in black except for a snow-white wimple and cap, just visible beneath her hood. She had shrewd, determined grey eyes which missed nothing, and which belied the softness of expression conveyed by her round cheeks, tip-tilted nose and generous mouth. 'I'll let him in.'

Cicely Ford managed to looked vexed, resigned and indulgent all at once. 'Dame Freda, it won't do him any harm to cool his heels a while until one of the servants is free to answer his knock.'

This, then, was the duenna employed by Edward Herepath as his ward's companion. I could not make up my mind in those first few minutes whether I liked her or not. I decided I should need to know her better before coming to any conclusion. Dame Freda gave me a slanting glance in passing and, ignoring her mistress's remonstrance, went at once to the street door and lifted the latch.

The young man who entered in a flurry of cold wind was typical of the dandies of his generation, and reminded me forcibly of Alderman Weaver's son-in-law as I had seen him three years previously. Once the sable-lined cloak had been discarded with an impressively negligent gesture, Master Robin, whoever he might be, revealed himself in all the glory of a parti-coloured doublet so short as to barely reach below his hips, thus displaying a padded cod-piece of impossible proportions, decorated with gold and silver tassels. His slender waist was circled with a belt of finest scarlet leather, which had a buckle studded with garnets and pieces of jade, and matching scarlet boots whose toes were at least two inches long – not, of course, as long as many shoe pikes, but certainly too long for general walking or riding. Both boots and belt hissed defiantly at the young man's shock of red hair, cut in a fringe across his forehead and curling to his shoulders. The eyes were hazel, set in a cherubic face of the extremely florid hue often found in people of his colouring. His whole bearing, reflected in his confident smile, gave me the impression of a man supremely sure of himself and of his welcome, totally impervious to the chilliness of Cicely Ford's manner towards him.

'Master Avenel,' she said quietly, making the slightest of curtseys and not offering her hand.

This, then, must be the son of the man who had bought the soap-works from Edward Herepath, and who, according to Margaret Walker, was sweet on Cicely Ford and probably hopeful of marrying her. I thought to myself that he hoped in vain.

I decided it was time to take my leave, and did so with as little fuss as possible. Muttering my farewells to Mistress Ford, I slipped back to the kitchen, where the housekeeper was still occupied with her cooking and too busy to give me more than a nod, and let myself out of the back door into the garden.

The stormy morning showed patches of radiance between the clouds, but it was still very cold, and I paused to wrap my frieze cloak about me and consider what I had learned. As far as the facts concerning William

Woodward's disappearance went, I knew little more than what I had already gleaned from Margaret Walker. I was, however, now aware that Edward Herepath was in love with Cicely Ford, and perhaps had been for several years, as was young Robin Avenel. I was also aware that Dame Freda greatly favoured Master Robin's suit, which suggested to me that she had been hostile to Robert Herepath; but then who, with Cicely's welfare at heart, would not have been? As for Robin Avenel himself, a man blessed – or cursed – with as much self-esteem as he seemed to possess, must have found it well-nigh impossible to understand Cicely's love for such a reprobate. He might have toyed with the notion that she was bewitched; that Robert Herepath had used a love potion or, worse, employed black magic to entrap her affection . . .

I caught my breath as I realized the direction in which my thoughts were leading me. I moved slowly along the garden path to the gate in the wall, where I paused yet again, one hand on the latch. I was beginning to see William Woodward's disappearance and Robert Herepath's execution not as two separate events linked only by the latter's cupidity, but as a diabolically cunning scheme to get rid of the younger man. And for what better reason than the love of a girl like Cicely Ford who, in one brief hour of acquaintance, had stamped her image so indelibly upon my own heart that I had desire for no other woman? Or, if not for her love, for her good, for the happiness which marriage to Robert Herepath would surely have denied her.

Once again, I brought myself up short. The deliberate abduction of William Woodward would have involved at least two other people, for it was impossible that William would have been a party to it himself; and a big, strong man as he was described as being, despite his advanced years, would not easily have been overpowered by a single person. Perhaps, after all, his story of being captured by Irish slavers was true, but instead of being paid to sell him into slavery, his captors had been bribed to murder him once he was set ashore in Ireland. Although he had been left for dead, the attempt on his life had been botched. He had been attacked in his house to leave plenty of blood and his hat thrown into the Frome in order to implicate Robert Herepath . . .

I lifted the gate-latch and stepped into the alleyway like a man sleepwalking, my thoughts in a turmoil. If any of these ideas had substance, then my clever schemer must have known of the money held in the cottage in Bell Lane, which brought Edward Herepath immediately to mind. Yet he surely could not have been the only person aware of his intention to be absent from Bristol on Lady Day and for the following night. A very little judicious questioning could have elicited the information, perhaps quite unconsciously given, that William Woodward had been instructed to hold the money until his master's return. It would be both foolish and perilous to jump to conclusions concerning the identity of the murderer, just as it would be equally foolhardy to presume my assumptions correct until I had more certain information to go on. In the meantime, after dinner, I would visit the Gaunts' Hospital and seek out Miles Huckbody, that sworn enemy of William Woodward.

I had just reached the end of the alleyway and was about to turn into Bell Lane, when I heard the rattle of a latch and then footsteps pounding the cobbles behind me. A second or two later, a hand roughly seized my shoulder, spinning me round with surprising force. I found myself face to face with Robin Avenel, his cheeks an even brighter shade of crimson after his effort to catch up with me. He had not bothered to put on his cloak, but he hardly seemed to feel the cold, such was his agitation.

'I've just been talking to Master Herepath,' he said, bringing his angry face close to mine, 'and I would advise you, chapman, to keep your nose out of what does not concern you!' His grip on my shoulder tightened. 'Robert Herepath was a wastrel and a scoundrel, and deserved a rope about his neck, even if he didn't murder the old man. I'm warning you! Don't dare to show your face round here a second time, harassing Master Herepath and above all upsetting Mistress Ford by raking over that unhappy business. What's done is done, and what happened was for the best.' He gave me a sudden shove which, because the cobbles were wet and slippery with filth, almost threw me to the ground.

Recovering my balance, I looked him straight in the eyes, my right hand clenched firmly at my side as I resisted the temptation to teach this conceited puppy a lesson he would not easily forget. Instead, controlling myself, I smiled and answered as courteously as I was able. 'I can give no such undertaking. I have Master Herepath's blessing to try to discover what happened to William Woodward, and the protection of Alderman Weaver. I bid you good-day.'

I swung on my heel and walked away, leaving him staring after me and, I hoped, discomfited, but also uneasily conscious that I could have made an enemy. It was as I was making my way up Broad Street towards the High Cross, that I recollected William Woodward had returned home wearing the clothes of a gentleman in place of his own homespun; a fact which seemed to render void my theory that perhaps, after all, he had been abducted across the water. I comforted myself with the thought that my inquiries had only just begun, and that the fragments of picture at present in my possession might yet come together to make a whole and reveal the solution to the riddle.

The midday meal was delayed somewhat, Mistress Walker having returned late from the dyer's with her basket of wool and, as a consequence, been late finishing her morning's spinning. When the wheel and spindle finally stopped turning, it was past noon, and as she ladled broth from the pot over the fire into the three wooden bowls on the table, I was aware that Lillis was covertly watching me.

'Did you visit Master Herepath, then?' she asked as her mother took her place alongside us. When I nodded, she continued, 'Did you learn anything new?'

I had my mouth full of bread, so was able to gather my thoughts before replying. 'No more than Mistress Walker had already told me.'

Margaret sighed, but without regret. 'I guessed it to be a fool's errand when you said that you were going.'

'Not completely.' I cleared my mouth with a draught of rough red wine, which Lillis had brought me from the vintner's. 'I learned your father had an enemy called Miles Huckbody, a pensioner now of the Gaunts' Hospital.'

Margaret laughed and shook her head. 'He'll do you no good. He could have had nothing to do with Father's disappearance. Oh, yes, he hated him all right, and possibly with good reason, but Miles Huckbody is too frail now to do more than eke out his days huddled over the fire in winter, or seated beneath the trees of Gaunts' orchard in summer.'

'Nevertheless, I shall visit him this afternoon,' I insisted.

Mistress Walker shrugged. 'You must do as you please, but I warn you, you're wasting your time.'

Lillis laid down her spoon, put her elbows on the table and propped her chin between her hands. 'And did you meet Mistress Ford?' she asked, with something so like a sneer in her voice that I felt my colour rising. 'Ah, yes! I can see you did, and have already fallen under her spell, like every other man. You are ready to spring to her defence if I so much as utter a word against her.'

'She is a lovely young woman,' I answered carefully,

anxious to conceal my feelings for Cicely Ford from Lillis's mocking gaze. 'Lovely in every respect, for she obviously has a gentle and loving nature.'

Lillis's face grew ever more cat-like as she slanted another look at me beneath half-lowered eyelids, lips parted to reveal small, even front teeth. 'Not like me, then,' she spat. 'My nature's neither loving nor gentle, but I'd fight tooth and nail for anyone I thought I loved. They'd not hang any man of mine without me moving heaven and hell to prove him innocent. And if I couldn't do that, I'd still try to save him by planning his escape. But these pious, prissy misses cave in at the first sign of trouble.'

'You talk like a child!' I exclaimed hotly, and noted with satisfaction how the blood stung her normally pale cheeks.

'Be quiet, Lillis,' her mother ordered. 'Roger is right. Cicely Ford is a lovely girl. Everyone knows it except you.'

'Including Roger himself, it appears.' Lillis got up and flung away from the table, going to sulk in a corner. Her eyes glowed redly and her mouth was set in a jealous pout.

'Take no notice of her,' Margaret told me. 'She gets these ill-humours now and then, and has done since she was a baby. Finish your soup and then you can be off, if you've still a mind to. As for me, I must get on with my spinning.'

Chapter Ten

The Gaunts' Hospital stands outside Bristol city walls and on the opposite bank of the River Frome, close by St Augustine's Abbey. Behind it, the ground rises steeply in the first of that series of hills which leads, eventually, to the high plateau above the great gorge, whose bed is that of the River Avon. The hospital itself consists of the church of St Mark, surrounded by hall, buttery, kitchen, dormitories and outbuildings. Its famous orchard stretches eastward until it almost abuts the land of the Carmelite friars, whose huge cistern has helped supply Bristol with its water for several centuries, piped across the Frome Bridge to the conduit by St John on the Arch. In spring, the orchard is a mass of foaming blossom, and in autumn the apples glow like round, red lamps among the leafy green; but on that cold January afternoon, the branches were bare and black, the grass at their feet yellowing beneath drifts of last year's leaves.

The porter at the gate listened courteously to my request before handing me over to one of the brothers, who conducted me to the hall, where many of the inmates were to be found. A fire burned cheerfully on the big hearth, flames roaring up the chimney, and stone benches, built along the other three walls, together with stools and trestles, provided seating for the fragile and elderly. Fresh rushes, mingled with dried summer flowers, were scattered across the floor, and helped to counteract the more unpleasant smells associated with extreme old age.

The man I sought, Miles Huckbody, pointed out to me by my guide, was not so very old, although I could have been forgiven for thinking him so on first acquaintance. His hair was almost white, the long, narrow face seamed and wrinkled. Before my arrival, he had been playing five-stones with one of his fellows, and I noticed how his hands shook as he rolled the pebbles. Having removed my cloak, I crouched down beside him and made myself and my business known. At the first mention of William Woodward's name, his features were contorted with hatred.

'That devil!' he exclaimed, and spat in the rushes. 'He had me and my family turned out because we'd fallen behind with the rent. He told me it was on Master Herepath's orders, but it weren't. Master Herepath knew nothing about it. William called in the bailiffs hisself.'

'You're sure of that?' I questioned, even though it tallied with Edward's own story. 'Without Master Herepath's authority, I doubt William could have done so much.'

'After I returned to Bristol, I saw Master Herepath in the street one day, and I caught at his bridle. I thought as you do, that William must've bin acting on his orders, but 'e denied it. Said 'e knew nothing about it 'til we were gone. Said William must've got him to sign the necessary paper by false pretences. Said as how William were over-zealous on his behalf.'

'And you believed him?'

'Why shouldn't I? He got me this place in the hospital because he's a friend of the Master Chaplain. Reckoned 'e owed me that much when 'e learned my woman and child'd died. I'd taken to begging in the streets and had this cough which 'as never left me.' He paused to give a demonstration, and indeed, the cough was bad, rattling in his chest and shaking his emaciated frame. ''E'd not have done that if he'd had ill intentions to'ards me in the first place.'

'But you were behind with your rent. Few landlords will tolerate that for long.'

'I'd never done such a thing afore. Always paid regular, but that quarter I'd bin ill and not able to harvest the crops, and the pig'd died.' He shrugged. 'My woman did her best, but she'd bin ill, too, and the little 'un was crying for food. What there was, we ate, so there was nothing left to sell.'

'You blame your misfortunes on William Woodward then, and no one else?'

'Ar, I do. That bastard!'

'You wanted revenge?'

Miles Huckbody eyed me askance as he suddenly realized where my probing was leading. 'I was glad to know someone had given 'im a beating, and gladder still to hear that he were dead, but 'twere nothing to do with me. Oo are you, coming here, asking me questions? I didn't prop'ly hear yer name, when you said it.'

'Roger,' I answered. 'I'm a friend of Mistress Walker, William's daughter. She's anxious to find out what really happened to her father during the time everyone thought him murdered.'

'Well, 'twere nought to do with me, but he were up to no good, you may be sure o' that. An evil man, if ever there was one.'

I made allowances for his antipathy towards William. It was natural that he should hate the man he regarded as responsible for the deaths of his wife and child; but I could not reconcile myself to the belief that William had had the Huckbodys evicted without orders from his master. And when, later, Edward Herepath had found himself confronted by the avenging figure of Miles, probably desperate enough by that time to commit violence, what more natural than that he should seek to lay all the blame on his rent collector? Conscience, too, sharpened no doubt by his growing love for Cicely Ford, may have spurred him on to make amends and obtain Miles a place at the Gaunts' Hospital. I sighed. Any faint hope I had nurtured that the man beside me had been in any way responsible for William Woodward's disappearance had been dispelled the moment I saw him. Margaret Walker had warned me that I was wasting my time, and she had been right.

I straightened myself and stretched my cramped legs with a regretful sigh. Miles Huckbody could not help me. His companion, who had moved a little distance from us when we began speaking, now came closer again, still holding the five stones in his hand.

'You be talkin' 'bout William Woodward and them Herepaths,' he accused us. 'My ears are sharp. I 'eard what you was saying.'

'No law 'gainst it that I knows of,' Miles Huckbody retorted. He jerked his head. 'This here's Henry Dando,' he informed me.

I nodded at the old man whose rheumy, pale blue eyes were regarding me so intently. Taking this as a sign of encouragement, he settled down again beside Miles on the bench and prepared to discuss the events of the previous year which had shocked all Bristol.

'Terrible thing to 'ave 'appened,' he said, ''angin' an innercent man.'

'Not so innocent,' Miles Huckbody protested. 'Stole his brother's money, rents and suchlike. Robert Herepath were always a nuisance, judging by all people do say of 'im.'

'Did you ever meet him?' I asked, interested.

Miles shook his head, but Henry Dando nodded eagerly. ''E were always around the city, kicking up 'is 'eels, even when 'e were younger, in trouble with the law, bein' bailed out o' the Bridewell by 'is brother. Once, 'e were in the Newgate lock-up fer three days fer knocking down an old woman in the street. And another time, 'e were in the castle cells a while after 'e and some of 'is friends

115

went on the rampage.' Henry sniffed. 'But 'is brother got 'im off each time. Knew the right people to bribe among the city fathers or in the sheriff's office. And it's no good you tut-tutting, Miles 'Uckbody, and trying to shush me, 'cause I knows what I know.' He sucked his few remaining teeth, probing with his tongue for lingering particles of dinner. 'I shouldn't think,' he added judiciously, 'that 'twere any great loss to Master Edward Herepath to be rid of 'im.'

Miles immediately sprang to his benefactor's defence. 'You mustn't say such things. They were blood-kin when all's said, whatever Robert may have done. Besides,' he went on, as though obscurely feeling that some kind of guilt were being attached to Edward Herepath, 'he were in Gloucester when it all happened.'

Henry Dando looked resigned. ''E were, that's true enough. I saw 'im meself on the Friday morning as 'e were setting out. 'E were some way distant, but I recognized that bay of 'is that 'e were ridin'.'

At this point, both men lapsed into silence, interest switching to me as two pairs of eyes looked me up and down. Their scrutiny rendered me uneasy. I thanked them for their help and swiftly took my leave before they could begin to ask questions. I also said my farewells to the porter at the gate before making my way back across the Frome Bridge and re-entering the city. I had learned nothing that I did not already know, but at least I was satisfied that Miles Huckbody could have had nothing to do with William Woodward's disappearance. I turned again to my belief that Irish slave traders could indeed have been involved, and decided that I would have to pay a second visit to Alderman Weaver. He appeared to know people who could advise me how to make contact with these elusive men, but it would have to wait now until the morrow. I was feeling suddenly very tired, with a curious lightness of the head and trembling in the limbs. Once again, I was forcibly reminded that I had not long risen from my sick-bed and, strong though my constitution was, I could not afford to overtax that strength. So instead of pausing outside the house in Broad Street, I continued past the High Cross, down High Street and across the bridge to the Redcliffe Ward and the homes of the weavers.

I ached in every joint, and could hardly wait for Mistress Walker to douse the rushlights and pull the curtain which divided the room in two before flinging off all clothes except my shirt, and tumbling between the blankets on my truckle bed. But once at ease, I found it unexpectedly difficult to sleep. To begin with there were small, rustling noises from the other side of the curtain as the women undressed, the subdued murmur of their voices as they said their prayers and bade one another good-night. Then, as silence filled the little room, the fire gave a dying spurt, sending shadows racing up the walls, to cling and then recede, merging into an all-enveloping blackness. Finally, as I thankfully closed my eyes, prepared for instant oblivion, a picture of Cicely Ford rose before me to set me tossing and turning restlessly, in the grip of unrequited passion.

I was astonished at the intensity of my feelings, of my desire for this girl I barely knew, of my longing to hold her in my arms and love her. The knowledge that I had no hope of ever possessing her in no way cooled my ardour; rather it made my lustful imaginings worse. These, no doubt, were further inflamed by the fact that I had not lain with a woman for several months; a celibacy enforced by the rough winter weather and my failing health. Now, however, in spite of recurrent bouts of weakness, I was on the road to recovery, and I had moreover met a woman who appealed to my senses as no other had in a very long time.

I had just decided that sleep would never come, when my eyelids began to grow heavy and my mind blurred at the edges, thoughts running together like melting ice. If I was conscious of the slender shadow which emerged from behind the curtain and tiptoed across the floor towards me, it was an awareness which failed to rouse me from the near-slumber into which I had fallen. It was only when I felt the chill of Lillis's naked body snuggling close to mine that I awoke to the full realization of what was happening. And by then it was too late. I was already on top of her, impelled by my craving for Cicely Ford.

It was over all too soon, and to my shame, I doubt if Lillis derived much satisfaction from our copulation – for to dignify it by any other name would be to lie – except that of having managed to seduce me in the face of my obvious determination to ignore her advances of the past few weeks. For if looks could have stripped me naked and put her in my bed, she would have been there long ago, in spite of my sickness.

I lifted myself off her and sat up, gasping, trying to keep the nausea from rising in my throat. I started to shiver, and only controlled it with an effort, clamping a hand across my mouth. She said nothing, but slender fingers, feather-light, stroked my back.

'Lillis,' I mumbled, turning towards her, but she hushed me, also sitting up and then sliding from the bed.

'It's all right,' she whispered. 'I know you were wishing I was Cicely Ford.'

Once again, she astonished me by her percipience, by the swiftness with which she could change from a greedy, grasping child into a woman of maturity and understanding. She made no further comment, but slipped away behind the curtain to resume her place beside her mother, who was snoring gently and sleeping the sleep of blessed ignorance. As for me, I was left to toss and turn upon my truckle bed for what seemed like hours, weighed down by a guilt which was not mine alone, but which felt, in the small hours of the morning, like a solitary burden. Resentment that I should feel solely responsible was intermingled with the knowledge that I had betrayed Margaret Walker's trust; that I had allowed my craving for another woman to overwhelm my senses. And my shame was compounded by the fact that Lillis had been a virgin; something, had I stopped to think about it, I should not have expected.

Eventually I fell into an uneasy sleep, and it was

already daylight when Margaret woke me. She had been up an hour or more, moving silently in and out of the cottage in order not to wake me. The fire was lit and an iron pot, filled with lentil porridge, was warming over it. Lillis, pale and withdrawn, was cutting slices from a loaf of black bread.

'Why didn't you wake me sooner?' I demanded ungraciously, stumbling out of bed and pulling my shirt down around my knees. I saw a faint smile lift Lillis's lips and hurriedly looked away again.

'I thought you could do with the rest,' Margaret Walker answered briskly. 'You looked tired last night. Take your clothes behind the curtain and dress.' She indicated a smaller iron pot. 'There's hot water if you want to shave before breakfast.'

Such kindness and consideration made me feel worse and, once behind the curtain, I sank down on the edge of their rumpled bed, burying my face in my hands. But it was too late for remorse and, in any case, I told myself sturdily, I was not wholly to blame. I must just make certain that it did not happen again. All the more reason, therefore, to fulfil my promise to my hostess and either discover what had happened to William Woodward during his mysterious absence, or admit defeat and then move on, as far away from Lillis as I was able.

Breakfast was a silent meal, all three of us preoccupied, Mistress Walker with the prospect of a day's spinning ahead of her, Lillis and I with our thoughts.

'And where do your inquiries take you today?'

Margaret asked me as she finished her porridge and rose from the table. 'Lillis,' she went on, 'I shall need you later to help me skein the wool and carry it to the weaving sheds, so don't go wandering off.'

Lillis, who was gathering up the dirty pots and plates ready to wash them, nodded silently. I had delayed shaving until after the meal, and was scraping at my stubbled chin with my black-handled knife.

'I'm away to see Alderman Weaver again, if I can. There's some information which I hope he will be willing to give me.'

As I spoke, I glanced at my discarded pack in the corner, and was seized with an urgent longing to be tramping the open roads once more, free of all obligations and relationships; free of love and shame and guilt; free of the ghost of a young man hanged for a murder he did not commit; free of the necessity to discover who had tried to kill a defenceless old man. I could almost feel the springing turf beneath my feet, the wind in my hair, the rain in my face. I could see myself opening my pack, the eager faces of the village women and girls as they clustered around me . . .

But I had once been trained for the monastic life, and in Chapter Sixty-nine of the Benedictine Rule it is set down that truth and justice are to be preferred before mere fallible inclination; and I had no doubt that God Himself had singled me out, as He had done on the past two occasions, for this present task.

Margaret noticed the direction of my glance and said

121

abruptly, 'You have no need to continue if you don't wish to. You're fit enough now. Get back to your peddling. I shan't hold you to your promise.'

Lillis had moved towards the door, needing to go to the well to draw more water for the dishes. As she opened it, she recoiled with a startled cry. A dead cat, rotten with maggots, had been laid across the doorstep.

'Has this happened before?' I asked, stooping to pick up the carcass by the scruff of the neck and throw it into the street sewer.

'Once or twice,' Margaret Walker admitted. 'Although who's to say it's deliberately meant for us? People have to dispose of their dead animals somehow.'

I made no reply, but knew that I must put aside all thoughts of escape for the present. My task was as yet unfinished and, however it ended, either in success or failure, I had not yet explored all the possibilities which might lead me to an answer.

Chapter Eleven

There was a certain impatience in Alderman Weaver's manner during my second visit, for which I did not blame him. He must have thought himself well rid of me after the first visit, and to find himself face to face with me once more only served to remind him how deeply he was in my debt. And no one likes to be under a permanent obligation, particularly to someone so inferior in station. I hastened to assure him that I should not trouble him again, and he instantly grew more affable.

'I should not have worried Your Honour now, but that certain information which has come my way leads me to believe that the Irish traders may have been concerned in Master Woodward's disappearance after all, and I wondered . . .' I hesitated, choosing my words carefully. 'What I would say is, Your Honour seems to have . . . connections with these, er, gentlemen. Would it therefore be possible for you to tell me where they might be found when in the city?'

The alderman looked taken aback. 'But I have already

told you,' he protested, 'that I have made inquiries, and no sighting of Master Woodward is remembered in Ireland.'

'You said you made inquiries of your friends. I should like to put some questions to the slavers themselves.'

Alderman Weaver appeared even more disconcerted, and drew closer to the fire for comfort. Outside, it was another dank and melancholy day, and through the glass windows I could see slivers of grey, monotonous sky. Walking here, in spite of my frieze cloak, I had been chilled to the bone.

'I did not say,' the alderman blustered, 'that I had any contact with the slavers! Merely that I know people who . . . who could have.' I made no reply, but looked steadily at him, watching the colour fluctuate in the puffy cheeks. After a few moments trying to outstare me, he finally gave in. 'Oh, very well! Perhaps I do know where they may be found. But I warn you, making contact with these men is a dangerous business. In the eyes of the law, they are criminals.'

I refrained from suggesting that they were probably also criminals in the eyes of God because, even then, young as I was, I had discovered that God's law and man's are not always the same: there are too many ambiguous answers to prayer for anyone to speak with confidence on behalf of the Almighty, one of the views which had set me at odds with the Church hierarchy and convinced me that I was not suitable for the monastic life. I said simply, 'I am prepared to take risks. And if I can call upon your name for protection, I think they cannot be too great.'

Alderman Weaver seemed to be both pleased and offended, each emotion struggling to gain the upper hand. Eventually, pride won as he looked through my eyes and saw himself as a man of the world, a person of influence with both high and low.

'Very well. There's an ale-house in Marsh Street. It has no name, but as you approach from the direction of St Stephen's Church, it will be on your right-hand side. It backs on to the great quay, not far from where the Frome runs into the Avon. The landlord is called Humility Dyson. Mention my name to him and ask for Padraic Kinsale or Briant of Dungarvon. If they're not there, he can usually tell you when they're expected. But take my advice, don't go at night and don't go unarmed. Do you have a cudgel?'

I nodded. 'It's with my pack at Mistress Walker's cottage. Thank you, Your Honour. I'll take up no more of your time.'

The alderman regarded me thoughtfully. 'You'll not discover anything, I'm afraid. I made very careful inquiries, as I told you. Whatever happened to William Woodward, he wasn't taken captive to Ireland.'

It was on the tip of my tongue to take him into my confidence, but I decided against it. He would only scoff at my theory of murder, for it might well implicate one of his friends or the son of one of those friends. As well to leave him in ignorance. So I thanked him yet again for his time and trouble, and left by the street door as, on this occasion, I had entered, much to the housekeeper's

indignation. But she made no formal protest; obviously
Ned Stoner had enlightened her as to the service I had
once rendered the alderman. A chill wind was sweeping
Broad Street and I drew in a breath of sharp, cold air.
The morning was beginning to gather pace and the bustle
of a large city, the second most important of the kingdom,
hummed in my ears. Carts rumbled past, making for one
of the city gates, laden with hogsheads of wine, bales of
cloth, crates of soap, south to Exeter, Salisbury or Southampton, north to Coventry, Chester or Norwich, following
the westerly trade routes into neighbouring Wales, in an
easterly direction to Oxford or London. Street-sellers were
abroad crying their wares, reminding me sharply that I
should be doing the same; shouts and halloos echoed from
wharves and quays as the dockmen unloaded ships
from Ireland, Cornwall, Spain, Italy, and even from far-
away Iceland.

I returned to Mistress Walker's for my dinner to find
Lillis absent. In answer to my query, I was told she had
gone to eat with Nick Brimble and his old mother, who
were both fond of her. I thought there was some slight
constraint in Margaret's manner and wondered, with a
sinking feeling in the pit of my stomach, if Lillis had
confided in her the events of the night. But when nothing
was said, I decided it must be a guilty conscience and did
my best to be cheerful, even ingratiating.

After some absent-minded chatter, I thought it wisest
to let Margaret Walker know where I was going, and
explained my morning's errand to Alderman Weaver. 'For

I think it possible that your father may have been carried to Ireland after all,' I said.

She glanced up from her plate, startled. 'You take care,' she advised me. Genuine concern for my safety showed in her face. 'That ale-house has a bad reputation. All the rogues and vagabonds of the city are known to congregate there. They'll cut your throat as soon as give you the time of day. I'm astonished that a man such as Alderman Weaver has intimate knowledge of it.'

I smiled at that. 'Men don't amass fortunes by being scrupulous about who they trade with,' I told her. 'You can't pick and choose in business and must go where there's money to be made. As for Myself, I shall take my cudgel with me; my Plymouth cloak, as they call it in the south. I'm big and strong and forewarned of possible danger. I can fend for myself.'

She frowned. 'You've been ill, remember, and still show signs of weakness now and then. Must you go? I thought Alderman Weaver had assured you, as I did, that my father could not possibly have been taken to Ireland. If that were so, why would he have returned wearing someone else's clothes?'

'That I don't know. But it seems to me that the slavers could have been paid to transport Master Woodward over the water and kill him, so that Robert Herepath might be accused of his murder.'

Margaret considered this for a moment, no trace of hostility now detectable in her manner. She was a quick-witted woman and immediately saw my meaning. 'But,' she asked, 'in that case, why not dispatch Father in the cottage and leave his body to be found?'

'Because it was necessary that the house should be empty when Robert went to steal the money. If he had seen a body, he could have abandoned his purpose and raised the alarm. On the other hand, if the murder had been delayed until after the theft, your father might have awakened and prevented it. So Master Woodward had to be removed, and his own story bears out the idea that he was taken to Ireland, just as his condition testifies to the fact that an attempt was almost certainly made on his life.'

Her frown deepened. 'But that points the finger of suspicion at Edward Herepath. He knew that Father was keeping the money for him until his return from Gloucester and, on his own admission, let the fact slip to his brother.'

'In itself a suspicious circumstance,' I pointed out, 'if you consider his reason for asking Master Woodward to guard his property in the first place. You told me yourself that Edward Herepath thought the money safer in Bell Lane than Small Street because, although he trusted his servants, he could not bring himself to trust Robert. Nevertheless,' I hastened to assure her, 'that does not mean I necessarily consider Edward Herepath guilty of the plot. There must have been others who knew of his absence from home; others to whom he or your father may have dropped a word, and one of them may have turned the circumstances to his advantage. Someone who hated Robert Herepath – and there seem to have been many such people.'

Margaret Walker bit her underlip. Her dinner had cooled, half-eaten, on her dish, and she pushed it aside. 'But who was to know for certain that Robert would steal the money?'

I shrugged. 'Everyone who knew him, I should fancy.'

There was silence, then she gave her head a brisk shake. 'My father wasn't taken to Ireland,' she said with certainty, 'and so you will discover, just as you will find this story of yours is a bag of moonshine. There's no connection but that of accident between my father's disappearance and Robert Herepath being hanged for his murder.'

I saw that there was no arguing with her in this mood. She had closed her mind to the possibility of being mistaken, and it was up to me to prove her, and all the others who agreed with her, wrong. I rose from the table and fetched my cudgel from its resting place, propped in a corner of the cottage beside my pack. As I once more wrapped myself in my cloak, Margaret spoke my name. I looked round, suddenly wary.

She had risen to her feet and was propping herself against the table behind her with white-knuckled hands. 'Roger . . .' She stopped, as if wondering how to continue. Then she said, 'Roger, Lillis is young for her years . . . irresponsible. She does not always foresee the . . . the consequences of her . . . her actions. But you are just the opposite. You have a wise head on your shoulders. I . . . I trust you.'

I could not meet her eyes. She was suspicious, but hoped that her suspicion was misplaced. Lillis had not said anything, but something in her manner had made Margaret uneasy. I mumbled a few words and hurriedly left the cottage, making my way back across the bridge and turning towards Marsh Street.

From St Nicholas Back, I walked through the bustle of Ballance Street, which skirts the great marsh itself, until I could clearly see the spire of St Stephen's Church rising above the houses. From there it was but a step before I swung left into Marsh Street, swarming as it always was at any time of the day with sailors, that fraternity of the sea who live largely by their own rules and pay little heed to the rest of us landlubbers. But they were not entirely lawless. I was later told that a levy of fourpence a ton on all cargo arriving at the port provided homes for a priest and a dozen poor mariners whose seafaring days were done, and whose prayers were offered regularly twice a day for all those still labouring upon the oceans. I wish I might have known it at the time, for my heart would not have hammered quite so fast as I crossed the threshold of the ale-house.

It was dark inside, there being no windows, only rush-lights and tallow candles which could easily be doused in the event of a visit from the sheriff or his sergeants. A beaten-earth floor was dotted with long wooden tables and benches, and casks of ale, two rows deep, were ranged against one wall. There was a second door opposite the one by which I had entered, opening on to the quayside. A narrow stone staircase led to the upper storey where, presumably, Humility Dyson lived. The landlord himself was a huge man in a leather apron, black-bearded and with arms on which the muscles were knotted like fists. Alderman Weaver had not described him to me, but his air of authority was unmistakable.

As I paused in the doorway, there was a disturbing quiet. Men who, a moment earlier, had been chatting with their fellows, fell silent, and all heads were turned in my direction. There was a definite air of menace in the room. I stood my ground, however, unable to see much at first in the sudden transition from light to dark, and tightened my grip on my cudgel, ready to lay about me if necessary. But gradually, as the drinkers took in my size and the way I was dressed, the babel of talk resumed. I was no longer being watched, at least not overtly; but I knew one false move would place me in immediate danger. I waited, therefore, until Humility Dyson approached me.

'And what's your wish, Master?' he grunted. 'Our ale's good, I grant you, but you'd do better supping at some of the other inns in the city.'

I ignored this unfriendly opening and said, 'I was recommended to come here by Alderman Weaver. He thinks you might be able to help me.'

Humility Dyson scratched his beard while looking me up and down. 'Alderman Weaver, is it?' he muttered presently. 'Well, and in what way does he think I can be of assistance?'

'I'm looking for two men, Padraic Kinsale and Briant of Dungarvon.'

The already small eyes seemed to contract with suspicion even as he watched me. 'What's your business?' he demanded.

'That's between me and them.' I hoped I sounded bolder than I felt. My palms were sweating and my hold on the cudgel was growing slippery.

I had no idea what I should do if he challenged me further, but after another stare he said grudgingly, 'Wait outside and I'll ask if they're willing to speak with you.'

My relief at finding the Irishmen present outweighed my uneasiness, and it was with a sense of elation that I stepped again into Marsh Street, letting the thick leather curtain which covered the doorway swing to behind me. A flock of seagulls swooped down, greedily pecking at the offal in the sewer.

After what seemed only seconds, the landlord pulled back the curtain and jerked his head. 'They'll see you. But watch your step, stranger. If this is a trick, you and whoever you've led here won't live to tell the tale.'

'I'm on my own,' I said. 'There's no one following me.'

Humility Dyson preceded me back inside. He waited a moment while my eyes grew accustomed once more to the darkness, then nodded towards a table in the furthest corner from the door, unlit even by a rushlight. I could just discern its outline and the shapes of two men sitting at it. No one looked up as I made my way between the intervening tables, but I felt as though dozens of eyes were boring into my back the moment I had passed.

Both Irishmen were completely in shadow, and it was

impossible to see either of their faces properly. After-wards, two pairs of glittering eyes and the brogue common to the area of southern Ireland, round about Waterford, was all that stayed with me.

'Well?' one of them murmured as I remained silent.

Now that the moment had come to speak, the folly of what I was doing swept over me: to ask two desperados if they had been paid to kill a man was the act of a brain-less idiot. But I have done that all my life, rushed in where angels will not tread, only to find the Devil at my heels. This time, fortunately for me, I was spared the necessity of putting the question into words.

'Humility says that Alderman Weaver sent you,' said the second man, 'therefore I think you must be asking about someone who disappeared and was thought to be murdered, but came back home as large as life. What was his name now, Padraic?'

'William Woodward,' I answered before the other Irish-man could open his mouth.

'So it was. Well, Master—?'

'Roger. Roger the chapman.'

'Well, Master Chapman, Alderman Weaver did right to send you to us, for although Padraic and I are not the only slavers working out of Bristol – there are plenty of Bristol men themselves playing the game – we being Irish know more of what goes on once the cargoes are deliv-ered, and have many contacts among both the men who run the markets and their buyers.' Briant of Dungarvon – for who else could he be, having addressed his friend as Padraic? – folded his arms together on the table and turned his head to face me more directly. 'So I say to you what we have already told the alderman, there is no trace to be found anywhere of anyone resembling this William Woodward. People would remember an elderly man with a broken head. No slaver could be rid of him.'

There was a soft chuckle from the other side of the table. 'I think our friend here,' said Padraic, 'might be entertaining the fancy that perhaps we were offered money to take the unfortunate man to Ireland and there dispose of him. Isn't that so, Master Chapman?'

'It . . . It had crossed my m-mind,' I stuttered.

'In that case,' Briant continued in the same gentle tone, but with such a hint of menace that my blood ran cold, 'you have the wrong men. We have our principles, don't we, Padraic?'

The other man nodded. 'We do that, and murdering someone in cold blood is not one of them. Of course, we can't speak for your fellow citizens, if it's a Bristol man you are, for in general they're a band of cut-throats. But think on this.' Padraic leaned towards me across the table. 'If the job was botched, as it must have been, someone somewhere along the coast surely had to see or hear something of a man wandering loose in such a state. And we tell you – ' he rapped the table to emphasize his words – 'at Alderman Weaver's request, and because he paid us well, Briant and I spent weeks, even months making inquiries for any sighting of this man, but no one, any-where, recalled seeing hide or hair of him. Not so much as a smell.' He raised his finger. 'So! We say again to you what we said to His Honour. This man, William Woodward, wherever else he was, was *never* in Ireland.'

Chapter Twelve

I believed them. Now, Ireland is a wild country, and how many miles have to be travelled, east to west, north to south, beset by how many dangers, I have no idea, but I was sure in my own mind that had William Woodward been taken there, he would not have wandered beyond the eastern seaboard or the confines of the English Pale. And it was these areas which had been scoured by Padraic Kinsale and Briant of Dungarvon, all to no avail. I considered the possibility that they were lying, but dismissed it: they had, as far as I could see, no reason to do so. They had no interest in the affair except a desire to oblige Alderman Weaver, to whom, no doubt, they owed some kind of debt. William Woodward must have needed succour and, furthermore, as he had managed to change his clothes, someone had to have knowledge of him; and if that someone lived in Ireland, surely Padraic and Briant would have flushed him out.

I decided there was no point in lingering. My informants had told me all they could and I had much thinking to do. I rose to my feet and bowed briefly to the two shadows in front of me. 'Gentlemen, thank you. You have told me all I wanted to know, and I shall not trouble you again.'

I was about to move away when one of them, Padraic I think, laid a friendly hand on my arm. 'A word of advice, chapman! Guard your back. Someone may resent you asking questions.'

The other man nodded. 'Disinterring old bones is a dangerous pastime. Take care.'

I repeated my thanks, this time for their solicitude, assured them I could look after myself, and took my leave, my passage to the door unmarked by silence or hostile glances. I had been accepted as harmless by the ale-house inmates. But once outside, in the gathering dusk of a late January afternoon, I leaned against the wall to catch my breath. I had been more nervous than I had realized. Phrases chased one another around inside my head; 'stirring up a hornet's nest', 'raking over dead ashes', 'disinterring old bones'. Maybe the Irishmen were right: perhaps I should look over my shoulder a little more often.

The thought, however, was ousted almost immediately by the need to reform my ideas concerning the possible whereabouts of William Woodward for those five months he was missing the previous year. If he had not been in Ireland, where had he been? Who had abducted him, and for what reason? Where had he been left for dead and who had come to his aid? My head was beginning to ache. A squall of icy rain blew in off the quay, making me shiver.

The sudden whiff of rotting fish turned my stomach and a cold sweat broke out on my forehead, reminding me yet again that I was still not as well as I should be.

My inclination was to go home and let Mistress Walker fuss over and feed me, but I balked at the thought of coming face to face with Lillis, who must by this time have returned from the Brimbles'. So, in spite of the increasing darkness and cold, I persuaded myself that another look at the cottage in Bell Lane, where William Woodward had lived, was not only necessary but also could not wait until morning. I wrapped my cloak more securely about me and, mindful of the recent warning given to me by the Irish slavers, grasped my 'Plymouth cloak' even more tightly in my hand.

Stalls and shops were beginning to close for the night as goods were removed from display and taken inside. Candles were lit in lamps and wall-sconces, and cressets hissed at their reflections in puddles underfoot. A few traders had already put up their boards and the streets were wearing a deserted air. Lights flared suddenly in windows, behind horned panes, and cobbles grew ever more treacherous as daylight waned. Twice I nearly slipped as my foot encountered some piece of slime which had missed the sewer in the middle of the street, and both times I just avoided falling. Common sense urged me to turn back towards the bridge, but once more, the thought of Lillis made me press stubbornly forward.

As I passed along Small Street, I saw the glow of light

from Master Herepath's house, and the idea of Cicely Ford, snugly within, made me breathless. My heart beat faster at the remembrance of her gentle face and quiet, dignified way of talking. It was with difficulty that I overcame my inclination to linger, like some love-sick youth, in the forlorn hope of seeing what might be her shadow outlined against the lighted panes. I forced myself to walk on, around the corner, into Bell Lane. Candles were lit in all the houses but one, which stood shuttered and empty, and which I guessed to have been William Woodward's cottage; or, to be more exact, Edward Herepath's cottage, which he had not yet rented out again.

Glancing round to make sure that I was unobserved, I tried the latch; but although it lifted, the door would not yield. I noticed a keyhole and realized that it was securely locked, but what else had I expected if the house was unoccupied? And why, indeed, had I come looking for the cottage at all? Hadn't it simply been an excuse for walking down Small Street so that, just for a moment, I could feel close to Cicely Ford? I was suddenly filled with contempt for my callow behaviour and hastened on along the lane.

I was so absorbed in my self-disgust that I walked straight past the entrance to Broad Street and suddenly found myself beyond St John's on the Arch, in Tower Lane. As, with a muttered curse, I pulled up short, I became aware of the muffled shifting of hooves and the snuffling of horses, accompanied every now and then by a soft whinny of pleasure. Glancing to my left, I saw the open gates and courtyard of a livery stable. At the same moment a man appeared, carrying two pails which he dropped with a clatter on the cobbles. They were plainly both empty, and I judged him to have been feeding and watering his charges before locking them up safely for the night.

I gave him 'good-evening' and he grimaced.

'It's going to be a cold night, friend.' He sniffed. 'It's drying fast, and I smell frost in the air. We've seen the last of the rain for a day or two, I reckon. Can't say I'm sorry. The dampness doesn't suit me. But I don't like the cold, neither. I'm away home as soon as I've locked up here, and if you've any sense, you'll do the same. I live in Wine Street. Stay a moment and I'll walk along with you.'

I shook my head. 'I missed my turning. I'm retracing my steps to Broad Street. I've lodgings in the Redcliffe Ward.'

'I'll still come with you. It's not very much out of my way.'

So I waited while he locked and bolted the big gates from inside before emerging from a wicket, which he also locked, going back twice to make sure he had done so.

'You're very careful,' I remarked as we turned into Broad Street.

He dragged the hood of his cloak over his head. 'You need to be nowadays, so many thieves as there are about. I don't know what the country's coming to,' he continued in a grumbling voice. 'It wasn't like it when I was a lad.'

It was on the tip of my tongue to suggest that his father

141

had probably made just the same complaint, but I stopped myself in time. Why waste breath in argument with a stranger, and one, moreover, I should utterly fail to convince? For judging by the thinning of his lips and the sour lines of his face, he was a man obsessed by the little unfairnesses of life, embittered by its petty irritations.

'You've been robbed yourself?' I asked instead, anticipating a reluctant denial. But I was wrong. As so often before, I had jumped to too hasty a conclusion.

'The stables were broken into one night last year and Master Herepath's bay was stolen.'

My attention quickened. 'Master Edward Herepath of Small Street?'

'Of course Master Edward!' The tone was short. 'That ne'er-do-well, Robert, never had the money to mount himself, and depended entirely for his horseflesh on his brother.'

'Was this theft before or after William Woodward's disappearance?'

My companion's head turned sharply towards me. 'Oho! You know about that, do you?' He shrugged. 'Well, and why not? 'Tis natural people still talk about it. A weird and terrible thing to have happened. And since you ask, there's no harm in telling you. Master Herepath's bay was stolen the very night that William Woodward disappeared.'

'The very same night?' I stopped dead in my tracks, although I was unaware of doing so until my new-found acquaintance twitched irritably at my cloak.

'Come along! Come along! It's almost dark and I don't fancy being abroad after dusk. Yes, yes! William Woodward and Edward Herepath's horse disappeared together. A fine, strong animal it was, too. Light bay with black points and a white snip between its nostrils.'

I resumed walking like a man in a dream, trying to assimilate this new fact and what, if anything, it might mean; by which time we had arrived at the High Cross and the parting of the ways.

'I'll bid you good-night then,' my companion said, turning left into the lower half of Wine Street. 'And if you're wise, you won't loiter. The city's plagued with thieves and footpads during the hours of darkness.'

He had hurried away before I could question him further, but at least I knew where to find him. And I consoled myself with the knowledge that I should have got very little from him then, anxious as he was to seek the safety of his roof before any dangers of the night befell him. I stared at his retreating figure for a moment before turning my feet towards High Street and the bridge.

I was first conscious of danger when I was almost half-way across the bridge, approaching the chapel of the Virgin. To begin with it was no more than the rising of hairs on the nape of my neck. I stopped and peered backwards through the darkness, but there was nothing to be seen except the row of houses and shops on either side of me. Nevertheless, I freed my right arm from the folds of enveloping cloak and renewed a tight grip on my cudgel. At the same time, I realized how deserted the bridge was in comparison with the other streets of the city. Here and there, a rushlight glimmered fitfully behind a window, but for the most part, the thrifty denizens of the bridge were saving their candles until later in the evening.

My friend from the livery stable had been correct, the weather was on the change; the dank mists of the past days were dispersing. A wind had arisen, tearing the pall of cloud to reveal, every now and then, a fugitive moon riding high in the heavens. In one of the gaps between houses, I caught a glimpse of the swift current of water, the reflection of a few lone stars caught in its ripples. The surrounding darkness was less dense than it had been, and shadows were more pronounced. Yet although I stood stock-still in the middle of the road, I could see nothing moving. With a shrug, I decided that my unease stemmed only from my imagination.

Foolishly, I had expected danger to come from behind: it had not occurred to me that any attackers might be lying in wait. I should, however, have thought of it, for there was no other route by which I could return to Redcliffe without going many miles out of my way. But it was only when I saw two bulky shadows fill the narrow gap between the chapel's outside wall and the house immediately facing it, that I realized my fears had been justified. It never crossed my mind that this pair of hired bravos could be intent on waylaying anyone but myself, and I was right. One of them raised a lantern to illuminate my face and immediately let out a yelp of triumph.

'It's him!' he exclaimed to his companion. And to me, he added, 'You've been long enough returning.'

I stepped back a pace, clutching my cudgel in both hands. 'How did you know I was abroad?' I queried.

'We asked at Mistress Walker's for you.' I saw the glitter of an already unsheathed dagger.

I risked a quick glance behind me, but there was still no one about. One of the men lunged and I parried the blow. I heard him curse violently, and it was obvious that he had not expected me to be armed with a stick. My assailants had anticipated, perhaps, a knife, such as some men carried for protection during the hours of darkness, but not a hefty cudgel. And a knife would have taken moments to draw, by which time they hoped to have dispatched me. I considered yelling for assistance – surely someone had to hear me in one of the shops or houses – but stupid pride would not allow it. How foolish men are when their courage is challenged! And how truly wise are women never to let such nonsensical notions get in the way of self-preservation.

Out of the corner of my eye, I saw the second bravo try to slip behind me, and I turned to face him before he could strike between my shoulder-blades. I released my cudgel with my left hand and swung it with all the force of my right at his dagger-arm. He saw the move coming and ducked, but not quite fast enough. The heavy stick caught him a glancing blow on his right cheek, making him stagger back, yelping with pain. I was unable to calculate how seriously I had injured him because the first man had already closed in, trying for the kill before I had time to regain control of my cudgel. He had an arm about my throat and I could hear his breath rasping in my ear.

I dropped my stick with a clatter and flung up both hands to free myself from his grip, twisting and writhing until I was bent almost double, dragging him down with me across my back. I could feel his muscles straining as he tried to straighten up and plant his dagger in my chest. He gasped out something to his companion, but I did not catch the words. The blood was drumming deafeningly inside my skull, and I knew that if I did not break his stranglehold in a second or two, I should lose consciousness and their work would be done. I was on my knees, still trying with all my might to prise his arm from about my throat, when I realized, with that animal instinct for danger, rather than by anything seen or heard, that the other man had recovered from the cudgel blow and was coming to help his fellow. I think I resigned myself in that instant to the fact that I was going to die.

I was unaware of the approach of my rescuer until a shriek like the wail of a banshee penetrated even my fading senses. My neck was released with a startled oath as my would-be murderer heaved himself to his feet. At the same moment, there was a rush of air as my abandoned stick was inexpertly and wildly sent flying in his direction, missing my kneeling form by inches and striking him, by the sheerest good fortune, full in the belly. Winded, he keeled forward, the dagger dropping from his hand as he clasped himself below the belt and started to retch. Dragging in mouthfuls of air which seared my chest like fire, I forced myself upright, and with my clearing vision beheld a small, whirling figure, hurling defiance at the two bravos and generally making enough noise to awaken the occupants of the neighbouring houses. Doors and windows were beginning to open, cautious heads peering out to discover the cause of the commotion.

'Help!' screamed Lillis. 'Murder! Murder! Murder! Somebody go for the Watch!'

My two assailants ran, the first man still bent double, clutching his stomach, but moving swiftly for all that, fear of capture making him show a clean pair of heels. By the time a small crowd had gathered around Lillis and me, he and his companion had vanished into the shadows at the town end of the bridge. There was little point in pursuing them, even had I wished it, for they would have disappeared into the maze of narrow alleyways surrounding the Backs, where such hired ruffians had their quarters.

Lillis fended off the growing circle of my well-wishers, many of whom were chorusing the usual litany about the dangers of the night streets and the general inadequacy of the Watch.

'Leave him to me. I'll see he gets home safely. He lodges with my mother.'

She picked up and handed me my cudgel, staggering a little under its weight. How she had managed to hurl it the way she did, I shall never know. Anxiety on my behalf must have given her the strength, just as it did when she slipped an arm around my waist and ordered, 'Lean on me.'

I laughed feebly. As we set off towards Redcliffe, with

cries of sympathy, commiseration and admiration for her ringing in our ears, I asked, 'What made you think I might need help?'

She snorted. 'I didn't like the look of those two men who came inquiring for you an hour or more since. And when you failed to return, I got worried and couldn't rest. I grew more and more convinced that some devilry was afoot so, in the end, I came to find you.' Her breath caught in her throat. 'I was afraid I'd find you dead.'

'I very nearly was. You arrived just in time. Thank you.'

She made no reply, supporting my flagging body as best she could until we reached the cottage, where Mistress Walker was keeping an anxious watch at the open door. She gave an exclamation of horror when she saw us and hastened forward to help me inside.

'What's happened?' she demanded, adding, without waiting for an answer, 'Sit down, lad. You look as if you're going to faint.'

And just to prove her right, I did.

Chapter Thirteen

I was dreaming. I was standing in the courtyard of the livery stables, and Edward Herepath was leading out a light bay with black points and a white snip between its nostrils.

The farrier was standing alongside him. 'No, no!' he was protesting. 'Henry Dando won't let you ride it on Thursday. He says it must be Friday because that's when he saw you.'

Edward Herepath pushed past him with an oath and, as he turned in my direction, his face became that of a much older man who, although I had never seen him, I knew instinctively was William Woodward. As I stepped backwards to clear a path for him and his mount, I noticed a cloaked and hooded figure standing at the stable gates, featureless, withdrawn. William passed the man without greeting, yet somehow I felt that they had met before, as an almost imperceptible nod of recognition passed between them. And then I saw that William Woodward had once again assumed the face of Edward Herepath. In the same instant, someone – the farrier I presumed – took a hold of my shoulder and began to shake me . . .

Mistress Walker was standing over me, a rushlight flickering in one hand, and behind her I could see Lillis's face puckered with anxiety.

'What's wrong?' I mumbled.

Both women breathed a sigh of relief. 'You were moaning and groaning so violently, we thought you must be ill.' My hostess placed the rushlight-holder on the table and felt my forehead. 'It's all right,' she said to her daughter. 'There's no fever. He must have been riding the night mare.'

'I was.' I sat up in my truckle bed, struggling to free my senses from the clinging remnants of sleep. I looked directly at Lillis. 'And you?' I asked. 'You're sure you've taken no hurt?'

She shook her head, and even through the gloom I could see that triumphant little smile which told me I was hers now: she had saved my life. And, far more than what had happened between us the previous night, the evening's events had put me for ever in her debt. I sighed and leaned back once more against my pillow. When she brought me water from the barrel near the door, I submissively raised my head and let her hold the cup to my lips; nor did I object when she kissed me lightly on the forehead. I noted the swift and curious glance that Margaret Walker gave me, but she made no comment, an omission which I found disturbing. It implied a tacit understanding between the two women.

Satisfied as to my well-being, they withdrew once more behind the curtain and retired to bed. I lay sleepless in the darkness, a prey to misgivings and fears for the future. If only it had been Cicely Ford who had come to my rescue, how happy I should have been then. But gradually, such ungrateful thoughts were replaced by the need to interpret my dream, for I knew from experience that somewhere in its jumble was a grain of sense. On only rare occasions in my life have I had what my mother would have called the 'sight', but whenever I am worried or perplexed, I have dreams which are so much confusion on the surface, but contain in their depths the seeds of truth. And whatever that truth might be concerning William Woodward's disappearance, someone had considered it worthwhile to have me murdered before I could discover it. Two ruffians had been hired to kill me and, but for Lillis's concern and bravery, I should now be lying cold and lifeless on the bridge.

I hurriedly put the thought from me and concentrated instead on my dream, going back over its events before it started to fade. Henry Dando! Who was he? I covered my face with my hands to block out the familiar shapes of the room, and tried to remember . . . Of course! Miles Huckbody's friend at the Gaunts' Hospital, who had mentioned seeing Edward Herepath. Now, what exactly was it he had said?

Miles had protested that Edward Herepath was in Gloucester the night William Woodward had disappeared. ''E were, that's true enough,' Henry Dando had answered.

151

'I saw 'im meself on the Friday morning as 'e were setting out. 'E were some way distant, but I recognized that bay of 'is that 'e were ridin'.' Yet surely both Mistress Walker and Edward Herepath himself had insisted that he had travelled to Gloucester on Lady Day; in other words on the Thursday. Either one was lying and the other had been misled, or Henry Dando had seen someone else riding Master Herepath's bay.

I eased my long limbs, uncomfortable in the narrow bed, conscious of a stiffening in the joints, legacy of my evening's encounter. With a sigh, I resigned myself to the knowledge that I should have to visit both the livery stables and Gaunts' Hospital again in the morning, and wondered how someone, somewhere, would react to the realization that I was not after all dead, but still intent on ferreting out the truth. In future, I must take my cudgel with me at all times when I walked abroad, and must also watch my back, as the Irish slavers had advised me.

I was beginning to doze once more when I recollected the cloaked and hooded figure, the man I had seen once and heard twice, and who had figured so silently in my dream. Who was he, and what, if anything, was his part in the mystery of William's abduction? And why, in that dream, did I get the impression that both William Woodward and Edward Herepath knew him? For a moment I was wide awake again, but fatigue and weakness exacted their toll, and the next thing I knew, daylight was filtering through the shutters.

The farrier was genuinely pleased to see me, and having

expressed the hope that I had reached my lodgings in safety the preceding evening – a hope I did nothing to dispel – he invited me into his room for a stoup of warmed ale. 'For it's a bitter cold morning, as I told you it would be.'

He rubbed his hands together and blew on his knuckles in an attempt to warm them. 'I said we should have frost and I was right. I generally am.'

I acknowledged this boast with what I trusted was an admiring smile, and indeed his prophecy had proved correct. The dank, cheerless streets of the past few weeks had been transformed by the heavy frost into a fairy world, all white and gold. Gossamer-thin clouds trailed each other across a pale blue sky; ice-bound streets glittered in needle-sharp sunlight; a thin coating of rime sparkled from every eave and post and wooden gallery. My spirits had lifted as I stepped out of doors, and every undertaking seemed less of a trial in the better weather.

I accepted the farrier's invitation and followed him into a small, single-storey building set in a corner of the stables. A row of six stalls housed, at present, only three horses, and a sleepy youth was just beginning his morning task of cleaning them out. He quickened his pace reluctantly at a command from the farrier, but, I suspected, dawdled again immediately we had disappeared from view.

'This is cosy,' I said, warming my hands at the brazier and noting with gratitude the jug of ale warming amongst its coals.

Wrapping a piece of cloth around one hand, my host

lifted the jug and poured its contents into two clay cups which stood on a side-table, one of which he handed to me. 'Now,' he asked shrewdly, 'how can I help you? For I don't flatter myself you've sought me out again after such short acquaintance just for the pleasure of my company.'

I was forced to admit that this was so. 'You mentioned that Edward Herepath's bay was stolen the night William Woodward was attacked and abducted. I am right, am I not, in believing that it was not the horse ridden by Master Herepath to Gloucester?'

The farrier put down his half-empty cup and wiped his mouth with the back of his hand. 'How could it have been?' he demanded irritably. 'Master Herepath set out in the morning. He asked me to have Cresside, his roan mare, saddled and ready for him as soon as possible after early mass.'

'So it was Thursday he travelled, not Friday? You're sure of that?'

My companion snorted angrily. 'Of course I'm sure. It was Lady Day and William Woodward came round later to collect the rent. This place,' he added by way of explanation, 'belongs to Master Herepath. He owns a lot of property in this city.'

'So I've been told.' I sipped my ale thoughtfully, wondering where this new fact fitted in among the rest. 'It was fortunate, at least, that it was one of his horses which was stolen. He didn't have to recompense another owner for its loss. How did the thief get in? The place is securely locked at nights from what I saw yesterday evening.'

'That it is!' the farrier replied with a fervour which made me suspect he might, at some time, have fallen under suspicion. 'Whoever it was, obtained a key to the wicket gate and unbolted the big double doors from within. Fortunately, I was able to call upon the witness of my neighbour to testify that I was at home all night. His wife was taken with labour pains shortly after Compline, and the midwife shooed him out of his cottage because he was getting under her feet. It was a long labour, being as how it was a first child, and he was so anxious, he and I sat up talking most of the night. It was dawn before the babe was born and I was finally able to join my wife in bed.' He added spitefully: 'She wouldn't do a good turn for anyone.'

'But your virtue was rewarded. You could not be accused of the crime.'

The farrier pursed his lips. 'Not of the crime itself, no. But Master Herepath and I are the only two people who are known to have keys to the wicket gate. I think the sergeant was inclined to think me guilty of complicity. However, Master Edward, God bless him, would have none of it, saying he would trust me with his life, let alone his horses, and sent the sergeant away with a flea in his ear. He's a good man, a just man, very different from his wastrel of a brother.'

'Was the bay ever found?' I finished my ale and returned the cup to the table.

'No. The animal completely vanished. After it was shut safely in its stall on the Thursday evening, it was never seen again to my knowledge.'

But it had been seen again, I thought to myself; on the Friday morning, according to Henry Dando; unless, of course, he had mixed up the days. It suddenly became imperative that I see him without further delay. All my curiosity was aroused. I thanked the farrier for his hospitality and said I had urgent business to attend to. I wrapped myself in my cloak, pulled the hood well forward about my face, seized my cudgel, and set out for the Gaunts' Hospital for the second time in three days.

Henry Dando was delighted to receive a visitor, and inclined to crow over Miles Huckbody once it was established that he was the one I wished to see.

'Why him?' Miles asked, aggrieved. 'Last time it was me you wanted to speak to. What have I done to displease you?'

'Nothing,' I assured him, 'and I'm delighted to renew our acquaintance. But something Master Dando said needs further explanation.'

Henry was none too certain that he liked the sound of this. 'Everythink I told you was true!' he said fiercely.

We were beginning to attract the attention of others in the hall, so I sat down on a bench near the fire, with him and Miles Huckbody on either side of me.

I turned to Henry. 'When we were discussing William Woodward's disappearance, you mentioned having seen

Edward Herepath on his way to Gloucester on the Friday morning, riding his bay.'

'An' so I did. Me an' a couple of others 'ad bin given permission by the master to hear mass at St Michael's. Gives us a bit of a walk, you see, an' we goes by the back roads, along Frog and Trencher Lane.'

'Which mass was this?' I asked. 'What time?'

Henry Dando pursed his wrinkled lips. 'Very early. Before breakfast.'

'Prime,' I suggested, and he nodded.

'That would be it. Well, after we'd left the church, we were coming down the 'ill, and we'd reached the corner of Magdalen Lane, when we sees Master 'Erepath on 'is bay a bit further along, turnin' up Stony Hill to'ards the windmill.'

'You're sure it was him? Did you see his face?'

''E were a bit too far off fer that, and the light weren't too good that time of a March morning, but I'd know that bay o' his anywhere. An' it looked like 'im.'

'But was it Friday?' I urged. 'Could you not be mistaken? Maybe it was Thursday you went to St Michael's?'

He gave me a pitying look. 'Thursday were Lady Day, weren't it? We'm expected to worship 'ere, altogether at St Mark's on any festival of the Virgin. Master Chaplain would never 'ave given us permission to go to St Michael's on the Thursday.'

Miles Huckbody concurred, adding, 'It was the Friday right enough. Henry and the others asked me to go with 'em, but I didn't feel like a walk. And 'twas the following day, Saturday, that rumours started flying about William's disappearance.'

'Well then,' I said to Henry, 'I'm afraid you were mistaken. It wasn't Edward Herepath you saw. He went to Gloucester on the Thursday and he was riding his roan mare. I have it on the authority of the farrier who runs his stable in Tower Lane. Furthermore, also according to the farrier, Master Herepath's bay was stolen sometime Thursday night or early Friday morning.'

Miles Huckbody broke into an unseemly cackle of mirth. 'I always said your eyesight's bad, Henry Dando, but you won't have it. Now p'raps you'll believe me.'

'Nothink wrong with my eyes!' Henry was belligerent. 'I could rec'nize that bay when I see 'un, don't you worry. An' 'twere 'im. As to it bein' Master 'Erepath – well, it looked like 'im, that's all I can say. If you don' believe me, ask the others.'

But the other three men who had accompanied Henry Dando to St Michael's Church on that March morning ten months ago had, when questioned, only hazy recollections of the horseman they had seen turning into Stony Hill from Magdalen Lane. Nevertheless, they were all agreed that it had been the Friday, and that Henry Dando had immediately identified the man and his mount as Edward Herepath and his bay.

'Which only goes to show that it takes fools to believe a fool,' was Miles Huckbody's disgruntled comment as he walked with me through the fields, back to the porter's lodge. His nose had been put out of joint by not being the chief object of my visit. I grumbled sometimes to myself that my life was too full of incident, but perhaps, after all, I was lucky: perhaps a full life was better than one which was too quiet.

'I think you do Henry an injustice,' I said. 'As I told you, the bay was stolen. Maybe the man riding him that Friday morning was the thief.'

Miles was sceptical. 'In broad daylight?'

'But it wasn't,' I argued. 'Mass was over, it's true, but it still wouldn't have been much after seven o'clock. Henry himself said the light wasn't good.'

'All the more reason not to believe the old fool.' Miles was determined to give his friend no credence. 'You'd do best to discount every word he says.'

We had stopped by the pigeon loft and I could hear the soft cooing of the birds within. The noise was soothing to my senses; I was still inclined to be jumpy after my encounter of the previous evening. I laid my hand on Miles Huckbody's sleeve. 'You and Henry have both been of great assistance,' I assured him.

'Not me. I've done nothing.' He was not to be mollified so easily and went on mockingly, 'The first time you came here, you thought I might have had something to do with William Woodward's disappearance, now didn't you?'

I smiled shamefacedly. 'Maybe. But not for long.'

'I wish I had,' Miles said viciously. 'The old bastard! In league with the Devil, he was.'

'Yet his daughter says he was a very pious man.'

Miles Huckbody looked at me, then grinned slyly. 'Oh,

ay! Daresay 'e might've been according to his lights. The weavers are a pious lot.' He chuckled throatily, but would say nothing more. Unsure of his meaning, I put it down to spite. Life had not been kind to Miles Huckbody; he was entitled to a little bitterness.

I took my leave, said my farewells to the porter at the gate, and made my way back across the Frome Bridge into Broad Street, and so home through all the bustle of midday to Redcliffe and my dinner. Until I had eaten and given sustenance to my great frame, I was unable to think clearly or reassemble my thoughts about what had happened to William Woodward. I had many pieces of the picture in my grasp, but not all of them. The truth was to be found somewhere, but there were parts of it I had not yet been able to discover. It only needed patience and time.

As I rounded the corner by St Thomas's Church, I paused, then stepped back hastily into the shadows. Emerging stealthily from the cottage opposite Mistress Walker's was the cloaked and hooded figure who had visited Jenny Hodge. As the door closed quietly behind him, he set off at a brisk pace in the direction of Temple Street.

Chapter Fourteen

I followed the cloaked figure as quickly as I could, but by the time I had crossed St Thomas's Street into Long Row, the man had vanished. There was only one conclusion to be drawn, that he had entered one of the houses. I glanced up and down the narrow alleyway, but there was no sign of life except for a thin dog scavenging among the rubbish, and two small girls bowling a hoop, crowing with laughter. It was dinner-time and most people were within doors. I approached the girls and asked if they had seen a man in a brown frieze cloak.

They both shook their heads mutely, but I had an idea that the younger of the two had been about to say something when the elder nudged her. There was that wary look in their eyes which one sees in children when their parents have demanded silence by threatening them with all the tortures of Satan if they disobey. I thanked them and turned back towards Mistress Walker's cottage in the shadow of St Thomas's Church. When I looked over my shoulder, the girls were still watching me, the hoop lying temporarily forgotten in the gutter.

I found my hostess in some distress with a bruised arm and wrist, because she had been jostled that morning in the market. Two young men, whom she identified as former friends of Robert Herepath, had deliberately bumped into her, sending her sprawling and spilling the contents of her basket. What she had found even more disturbing was how reluctant many of the onlookers had been to come to her aid.

'Fortunately, Nick Brimble and his mother happened along at that moment, and helped me up, and the tailor let me sit down for a while inside his booth.' She smiled bravely. 'So I'm none the worse for wear. But it shows that some people still think I know what happened to Father, and that I may even have had a hand in his disappearance.'

'That's nonsense,' I said stoutly, taking my place at table. 'How could anyone imagine that his own daughter would beat and abduct an old man, even if you had the strength, which you so obviously have not.'

She put dishes of salted herrings in front of me and Lillis, for the day being Friday we were eating fish, and added another of oatcakes in the centre of the board. Then she took her seat alongside her daughter.

'Of course no one would think such a thing,' she chided me, 'but there are those who believe that Father arranged his own disappearance for some secret purpose of his own, and that I helped him.'

'But the blood,' I protested. 'The bloodstains you found

in the cottage, how do they explain those?'

She shrugged. 'Maybe he cut himself, his wrist perhaps, and let the blood drip on the bedcover and the rushes.'

'How much blood was there?' I sucked some herring bones from between my teeth and spat them out on the side of my plate while waiting for her answer.

'There were two large stains on the bedcover and quite a number on the floor. There were also some splashes on the walls, and hand-prints around the wall-cupboard.'

'A lot of blood then; more than a man could afford to lose if he intended going on a journey.' She glanced inquiringly at me and I said with some impatience: 'If he disappeared, as he did, he had to go away, and far enough away that he couldn't easily be found. He wasn't hiding in the city. In those circumstances, he wouldn't weaken himself so much that he was unable to walk, or even to ride if he could find a mount.'

As I spoke, there flashed into my mind the picture of a man on a stolen horse turning from Magdalen Lane into Stony Hill, towards the windmill. I stared into space, transfixed by the image thus conjured up, feeling as though I were on the brink of a revelation. I was about to make a significant discovery, only Lillis's sly laugh interrupted my thoughts before I could do so.

'You look as though someone had gutted and then stuffed you,' she remarked unkindly. 'And you haven't said anything about my hair.'

Her mother smiled. 'He hasn't even noticed. And you

163

going to the market specially this morning to buy those ribbons!'

I saw then that Lillis had discarded the triangle of cloth which she normally tied around her head in the daytime, and the thick coils of hair had been allowed to hang down in two braids, each one decorated with a bow of red silk.

'It looks very pretty,' I said lamely. But the sight of the ribbons reminded me sharply of those tucked away in my pack in the corner, and the need, before my store ran out, to start earning some wages. I could not continue to live off Mistress Walker: my pride would not allow it.

Lillis could see from my expression that her brave attempt to capture my attention and wring from me some small, pathetic compliment, had failed. She said nothing further, but lowered her eyes and began to eviscerate her herring with a quiet fury.

I made a feeble attempt to placate her. 'I should have noticed,' I apologized. 'But you shouldn't have wasted your money. I have ribbons in my pack. You need only have asked me.'

She dropped her knife with a clatter and bounced up from her stool. 'I'm not hungry,' she announced. She strapped on her wooden pattens and found her cloak. 'I'm going to see Nick and Mistress Brimble. Nick, at least, won't fail to notice.'

There was a blast of cold air as the door opened and closed behind her. After her departure, there was an awkward silence. Mistress Walker said quietly, 'She's fond of you, Roger.'

I pushed my herring around my plate, my appetite deserting me. 'I know. Mistress Walker,' I continued hurriedly, desperate to avoid any further discussion of the matter, 'we were talking about your father; about the possibility that he could have arranged his disappearance himself. If I have asked you this before, forgive me; but do you know of any reason why he might have done so?'

'No. None.' She spoke decisively, accepting for the moment that I had no wish to pursue the subject of Lillis, although I had no doubt that in her own mind it was far from closed. 'Moreover, my father returned home, bearing the scars of a terrible beating. He had, sometime previously, been horribly injured, injuries which he could not possibly have inflicted on himself. I think you will have to look elsewhere for a solution.'

I thought so too, and said no more, asking instead, 'Who is the hooded man I've seen twice now, once at Burl Hodge's cottage and again this morning leaving a house close by? I am almost certain, too, that I heard his voice at your door the second or third night I was here, when I regained consciousness for a moment.'

There was a pause so slight I could well have imagined it. Then Margaret Walker answered smoothly, 'Many people are abroad in the streets, and at this time of year anyone with any sense is well wrapped up against the cold. You yourself, when you returned before dinner, had your hood pulled forward about your face. As for anyone who may have called here during your illness, it is a week or so past, so how can I remember? Lillis and I, in spite of our difficulties, are not completely friendless.'

'It was dark. After curfew, when fewer people risk the streets, especially in winter. Furthermore, this was not a friend. You spoke angrily to him, telling him to be about his business and threatening to send for the Watch.'

A little colour stole into her sallow cheeks, but her gaze did not falter. 'Oh him,' she said. 'An old acquaintance of my father, and one I always considered to have a bad influence on him. I want nothing more to do with him now that Father is dead.'

'But why would he continue to trouble you?' I persisted, and had the satisfaction of seeing a hunted look in her eyes.

But again, she answered easily enough. 'Perhaps he is lonely.'

'But from what I have seen, he appears to be welcome in many of the weavers' cottages in Redcliffe.'

Margaret began gathering up the dirty dishes, stacking them at the end of the table near the fire, where water was heating, ready to wash them. Keeping her hands busy helped to steady her voice. I heard only the faintest of quavers as she said, 'That's nothing to do with me. Folks look to their own affairs round here. I can only say I don't like the man, nor do I want him in my cottage. Are you sure it's the same person you've seen on each occasion?'

'I recognized the cloak. Very mud-stained and torn around the hem, as though he does a lot of walking.'

'That could be true of almost anyone hereabouts. Weavers and spinners do not have the means to travel on anything but Shank's mare.'

I shook my head. 'No, Mistress Walker. You knew at once who I was speaking of the moment I mentioned the man in the cloak. There is something you're keeping from me, and you won't tell me what it is. If you want me to discover the truth about your father, that's unfair.'

'Nonsense!' She clattered the dishes angrily. 'It has nothing whatever to do with Father's disappearance. I told you, the man's just one of his friends; a man I dislike and want nothing more to do with. Move, lad, move! I must get on. I have to take a load of yarn to the weaving sheds this afternoon.' I saw that it was useless to pursue the matter further, for I should only get the same dusty answer. I rose from the table and picked up my pack, slinging it over my shoulders. 'What are you doing?' she demanded sharply.

'I'm going to earn some money if I can. This is my trade.' I settled the pack more comfortably. 'Moreover, a little honest work will do me good and help me think better. Don't worry. I shall take my cudgel with me.'

She said with some constraint, 'There's no need for that. I didn't mean to reproach you just now, nor to sound ungrateful.'

I smiled and, suddenly moved by a kind of tenderness for her, kissed her careworn cheek. 'Nor I to sound churlish. But I meant what I said. A little honest toil will do me good.'

She sighed. 'You'll need a permit, lad, to trade within city limits, or you'll have members of the City Commune on your tail. Bristol money stays in Bristol pockets, that's something you'll have to learn. And I doubt if they'd grant permission to a stranger. Now, if you were going to make your home here, or were married to a Bristol girl . . .' Her voice trailed away into silence, but it was a silence that shouted aloud an unspoken question. She regarded me, her head on one side.

I slipped the pack from my shoulders without giving her an answer. 'That's that, then,' I said dejectedly. 'But I must walk to clear my head. I shall be back before it's dark.' And I went out, leaving her standing in the middle of the room, a defeated look in her eyes.

I walked quickly, swinging my cudgel, trying, with my purposeful strides, to shake off a sense of frustration; a feeling that events were closing in on me; of being caught in a snare. It was not that I did not wish to get married one day, to have children and a home. The words of the Carmelite friar in the barn near Salisbury came back to me. 'The best thing you can do, my son, is marry. Find a good woman who will make a home for you to go back to every winter, and who will maintain it while you are away each summer.' Sensible advice if I could find the right woman, but that woman was not Lillis. There was something wild and fey about her which frightened me. And, as so often lately, my thoughts turned to Cicely Ford.

But I had no illusions. She was too far above me even if she had loved me, which she did not. How could she? We had only met once; yet it was not that. No man now would ever obtain the heart of Cicely Ford. Her hand, maybe, but her heart was in the grave with Robert Herepath, and her life, however long or short it was, would be an atonement to his memory for doubting him.

I had been so engrossed in my thoughts that I had not noticed where I was going. I was half conscious of the people around me, of blindly bumping into someone every now and then, of being cursed and told to watch my step. But I had walked down Broad Street and was half-way across the Frome Bridge before a gentle voice, calling my name, made me aware of my surroundings.

'Master Chapman.' A hand was laid on my arm as a slight figure barred my path. 'Where are you off to in such a hurry?'

I blinked, like a man in a dream, for there before me was Mistress Ford herself, wrapped in a blue woollen cloak, the silk-lined hood framing her charming face, into which a delicate colour had been whipped by the wind. Behind her, a disapproving frown marring her pleasant features, stood her companion, Dame Freda.

'I . . . I don't know,' I answered stupidly. 'I . . . I was just walking.' I felt myself blushing. She must think me the biggest fool in Christendom.

But she gave no sign of being aware of my discomfiture. She simply smiled her sweet, grave smile and said, 'In that case, would you be kind enough to turn back and give me your support as far as Small Street? I'm rather tired, and Dame Freda, as you see, is weighed down with the basket.'

I barely registered her companion's outraged expression or her breathed remonstrance of 'Cicely!' My heart was beating too fast to have thought to spare for anything but my own turbulent emotions. Would I be kind enough? *Kind* enough! Did she not realize that I would go with her to the world's end?

'O-Of course,' I stuttered, and she laid one hand on my proffered arm.

'Dame Freda and I have been visiting the House of the Magdalen Nuns,' she confided as I retraced my steps back across the bridge to St John's Gate. She indicated the full basket carried by the older woman. 'As you see, they always load us with gifts. Today it's wine and winter vegetables from their garden.' A faint sigh reached my ears. 'They have been so good to me, particularly Mother Superior, since . . . since . . .' Her voice broke and she was unable to finish. After a moment, she continued more cheerfully: 'The hours I spend there are such happy ones. It is a house of retreat, you know, for women, and also a seminary for young ladies who can afford it. The young girls are so gay and carefree.' She spoke as though she were fifty at least, instead of the seventeen or eighteen summers I took her to be. She added, almost to herself, 'There must be great satisfaction in the religious life.'

Dame Freda, however, had caught her meaning if not her words. 'As great a piece of nonsense as ever I heard!' she exclaimed angrily. 'You were made for marriage and children. Sorrows fade, believe me. You'll fall in love again sooner or later. There are plenty of good fish in the sea.'

I thought Cicely Ford might take umbrage at being addressed in such round terms, but she merely turned her head to smile at her companion. Her tone, when she answered, was even amused. 'And Master Avenel, I suppose, is leader of the shoal! Dear Dame Freda, I appreciate your concern for me, but I shall never love Robin Avenel.'

She said no more on the subject; but, as an outsider able to see the truth more clearly than those closer at hand, I realized at once that Cicely Ford had already made up her mind. She may not have known it herself just then, but her future lay in the cloistered calm of a nunnery and a life devoted to helping others. She would become a Bride of Christ, but of no earthly man. I think my wild and ridiculous passion for her started to fade from that instant. In my eyes, she began to assume an aura of sanctity which ordinary love could only despoil.

We had passed beneath the arch of St John's Gate and turned right, along Bell Lane.

'We will use the back entrance,' Cicely decided. 'We'll take the basket directly to the kitchen, and Mistress Hardacre can then dispose of our plunder as she sees fit.' A dimple peeped as she glanced up at me, smiling. 'Master Chapman, I have imposed on you shamefully. There is no need for you to come any further. Leave us here and go your way.'

I shook my head. 'I shall accompany you to your gate,' I insisted. 'The back lane is stony, and in your present state of fatigue, you might well stumble and hurt yourself.'

She accepted my offer with gratitude, and we directed

our feet along the narrow alleyway behind the Small Street gardens. We were a few paces from the third gate in the wall, when it opened and a figure emerged; a man's figure, shrouded in a heavy brown frieze cloak, torn and muddy about the hem, the hood pulled well forward across the face. I must have exclaimed, for his head turned briefly in our direction before he walked swiftly away from us towards the other end of the alley, which opened into Corn Street.

'Who was that?' Dame Freda demanded indignantly.

Cicely Ford was untroubled by the stranger. 'It will be one of Edward's supplicants. No one who comes to him is ever denied help. The net of his charity is cast wide. Master Chapman.' She took her hand from my arm. 'Thank you for your assistance. I shall remember you in my prayers. Come, Dame Freda, we must go in. Edward will be wondering what has happened to us. I stayed longer with the nuns than I meant to.'

With another grateful smile, she and her companion passed through the gate which I was holding open, and vanished inside. I closed the weighty, iron-studded, wooden leaf behind them and leaned against the wall, my heart thumping excitedly. The hooded man had at last provided me with another link, besides the obvious one of master and man, between Edward Herepath and William Woodward.

Chapter Fifteen

So rapt was I by this discovery, that it was several moments before I realized that I was allowing my quarry to escape. I set off immediately along the alleyway as fast as my legs would trot, in the direction of Corn Street. Emerging into this busy thoroughfare, I stopped and looked about me.

The afternoon was well advanced by now, but it was not yet dusk and the street was still full of people. Close beside me, a draper's stall was stacked with rolls of cloth; blue, scarlet, green and purple cascaded from shelves lining the booth. The owner, seeing me pause, tried to interest me in his wares, offering me a fine Italian velvet at twenty shillings an ell. I shook my head, indicating with spread hands that my pockets were well and truly to let. The draper shrugged and turned to look for a more promising customer.

It seemed a hopeless task, trying to find the hooded man in such a crush of people, but suddenly I saw him. He was on the opposite side of the street, standing in the opening of an alley which led to the church of All Hallows. He appeared to be deep in earnest conversation with another man dressed in a thick jacket and hose of grey homespun. As I watched, the two walked deeper into the shadows. There was something conspiratorial in their manner which intrigued me. I crossed the road, dodging between several carts piled high with goods and a lady's painted wagon. The savoury scents from a nearby cookshop wafted about my nostrils.

As it happened, the cook-shop stood close by All Hallows, on one corner of Corn Street and the alley. I stopped to buy myself a pie and, whilst doing so, was able to locate two shadowy forms sheltering in the porch of the church. Biting into my pie, I risked a swift, sidelong glance as I passed, but neither man noticed me, so intent were both on what they were discussing. A few paces further on, I stopped and sidled back again, keeping as close as I could to the church wall. Fortunately, not only was the side-street dark, but the light was also fading as the winter day moved towards mid-afternoon. The bright promise of the morning had not been fulfilled.

I crammed the last of the pie into my mouth and flattened myself against the outside of the porch. Although they were whispering, I could hear what the two men were saying quite distinctly. It needed only a minute or two before the mystery of the hooded man was made plain.

'If a man truly repents his sins, there is no need for confession. Absolution from a priest is a mockery and damnation.' I recognized at once the deep voice, with its slightly rasping tone, that I had heard in Jenny Hodge's cottage and at Mistress Walker's door. 'For every man shall be condemned by his own guilt and saved by his own merit. It is impossible for his wrongdoing to be forgiven by another, be he the anti-Christ himself.'

I heard the second man shuffle his feet. 'If you mean His Holiness the Pope . . .' he was beginning, when he was interrupted.

'I tell you no man on this earth should be received as Pope! We should all live after the manner of the Greek Church, under our own laws! No true-born Englishman should be controlled from Rome. And what of priests who have themselves committed mortal sins? Are such men fit to administer the Sacrament? What a travesty is made of justice when they can shelter beneath the Church of Rome and their crimes go unpunished!'

'I have . . . thought on these things,' the man in grey homespun admitted after a moment's silence.

'Then join us,' the hooded man urged, 'at one of our meetings, when better men than I will expound our doctrine more fully. There is a cave in the great gorge, which cuts through the downs outside the city, where a number of us meet once a month on a Wednesday.'

'I'll think about it,' the second man promised, 'but it won't be easy getting away from my wife without her asking questions. She's not of my persuasion. A devout woman, always on her knees in church.'

'The righteous will find a way,' the hooded man assured him. 'Meantime, stay clear yourself. Remember the words of John Wycliffe. "Splendid buildings and gaudy decorations draw away the mind of the worshipper." '

There was another pause before the man in grey homespun murmured on a note of query, 'The changing of the bread and wine . . . This, too, troubles me.'

'It troubles many of us,' his mentor whispered back. 'Bread is bread and wine is wine. They cannot turn into flesh and blood because a priest utters a few words of consecration over them. The body of Christ may be present at the Eucharist, and may be present in you *as well as* the bread and wine, but that is different. The doctrine of transubstantiation confers upon priests the importance of powers which they do not in fact possess. Which no man possesses.'

I had heard enough, and decided that it was time I moved before they discovered my presence. I detached myself from the porch wall, slipped between the neighbouring houses into Cock Terrace, and from there made my way by St Nicholas Street and St Nicholas Back to the bridge. Instead of immediately crossing into Redcliffe, however, I leaned on the harbour wall, staring into the muddy depths of the Avon.

So, my hooded man was an itinerant Lollard preacher, travelling his allotted ground, gaining new converts where he could and holding secret meetings for those already of his persuasion. He may once himself have been a priest, but the Lollards set so little store by the priesthood and the laying on of hands that many of them are laymen. I blamed myself for not having suspected the truth, for

Bristol is a notorious hotbed of religious dissension. I do not know why this should be so, for it is still as true today as it was in times past; and also, again for reasons I do not understand, weaving communities throughout the kingdom have always been great followers of Wycliffe.

I had been watching the dark, melancholy flow of the river for some moments before the full meaning of my discovery struck me. Jerking upright with an exclamation which startled two young anglers further along the wall, I realized that both William Woodward *and* Edward Herepath must be of the heretical persuasion. Margaret Walker had assured me that her father was a pious man, but there had been that in her voice which had puzzled me. Moreover, I had been convinced all along that she was guarding a secret, and now I knew what it was. I suspected that she had violently disapproved of William's beliefs, not because she was a good daughter of Holy Church, but because of the threat they posed to herself and Lillis. If the truth had been discovered, not only would William Woodward have been burned at the stake, had he not recanted, but suspicion might well have attached itself to his family. Alderman Weaver would have had little compunction in turning the women out of their cottage.

Many Lollards had been executed since the heresy first took root in the previous century, and among them had been men of note. The most famous had been Sir John Oldcastle, friend and companion of the great Harry of Monmouth himself, but that had not saved him. And his standing in the community would not save Edward Here-path if his beliefs ever became generally known. It might explain why he had allowed such licence to his brother; why a respectable man had cosseted and protected such a wild young reprobate as Robert Herepath seemed to have been. But if Robert had a hold over him, that would be the explanation.

I turned and made my way slowly back to the bridge. On this occasion there were still plenty of people about, and a few patches of blue sky were visible between the gathering clouds. But there would be no frost tonight, and the air was less chill as the rain squalls swept up-river from the sea. I thought again of Edward Herepath, but this time of his connection with William Woodward. If they had met, as they undoubtedly must have done, during one of those secret meetings in the cave in the gorge, then they may well have struck up a friendship which had resulted in William being offered the job of rent collector. If he had confided in Edward his dislike of weaving, his belief that he had been unfairly treated by the Weavers' Guild, the younger man may have felt an obligation to assist him when the opportunity arose. For in my experience, shared beliefs make stouter friends and firmer allies than any ties of blood.

I had learned something that afternoon which put me one step forward on the road to the truth, and I felt a momentary glow of satisfaction. But was it a step in the right direction? Did my discovery have anything to do with William Woodward's abduction and reappearance?

The glow faded and died, leaving me feeling suddenly careworn. My powers of deduction were failing me.

The bell was ringing for Vespers as I passed St Thomas's Church and I went in to stand among the rest of the people thronging the nave. I realized that I had not been to mass for several days, and the omission worried me. I was too lax, I told myself severely, at the same time wondering why I was suffering this attack of conscience. Was I bothered by the conversation I had overheard? Did I find myself in secret agreement with many of the Lollards' arguments? I crossed myself hurriedly, but was unable to rid my mind of heretical thoughts.

Transubstantiation or consubstantiation, who was right? And were there older powers even than Christianity that struggled to make themselves felt? Often, walking through silent stretches of forest, particularly the oak and beech woods of our Saxon forebears, I have been aware of an alien presence: Robin Goodfellow, perhaps, or Hodekin the wood sprite, or the most terrible spirit of all, the Green Man.

Margaret Walker was just finishing her afternoon's spinning when I entered the cottage, but there was still no sign of Lillis. 'You'll be wanting your supper,' she said. 'You look tired out.'

I took off my cloak, propped my cudgel in a corner, and sat down on a stool close to the fire, spreading my hands to the blaze. I said nothing for a while, watching her coil the spun yarn into a basket and pile the raw wool into another. This latter had already been dyed red, a colour for which Bristol cloth is famous: 'red raddle' I had heard Mistress Walker call it, and she had explained that the dye was found, running like veins, through rocks.

When she had finished her task, she straightened her back and regarded me, hands on hips. 'You're very silent. You're not still holding what happened at dinner-time against me? I'm sorry if I was cross, but we all get out of sorts sometime.'

I raised my head and looked her full in the eyes. 'The hooded man, who was a friend of your father's, is a Lollard preacher. Master Woodward was of the same persuasion.'

I did not pose it as a question, I was too sure of my ground for that, but she treated it as one. 'No, of course he wasn't! How can you ask such a thing?'

'He's not asking, Mother.' There was a sudden blast of cold air, and Lillis stood on the threshold. She came further into the room, closing the door behind her, and stooped to take off her pattens. Her cloak she tossed on to the table. 'Yes,' she said to me, 'my grandfather was a follower of John Wycliffe.'

'In God's name, girl!' Margaret Walker seized her daughter's arm. 'Don't you realize how dangerous it is to admit such a thing? And you!' she added fiercely, turning her eyes in my direction. 'Making such accusations! Supposing it had been someone other than Lillis who just came in? They could have heard you as well as she did. Do you want to get us turned out of this cottage?'

'I'm sorry,' I said, 'but I must know the truth. It may have something to do with your father's disappearance.'

'Nonsense! How could it?'

I shrugged. 'I don't know that yet, but I told you at the start, I needed to know everything about Master Woodward.'

Lillis tossed her head. She had freed her hair from its silken bows and let it loose in a jet black mane. 'I would have told you,' she assured me scornfully. 'Besides, so many of the weavers are Lollards, there's no need to be afraid.'

'And many aren't,' her mother retorted. 'And there are those who wish us harm. One whisper of your grandfather's heresy and they would carry the tale straight to the alderman. If you wish to be turned homeless on to the streets, I don't.'

I intervened quickly before Lillis could reply. 'You have no cause to fear me,' I said quietly. 'You know I would never hurt you. But in fact, you need say nothing. I know that Lillis is telling the truth.' I suddenly remembered something. 'There was a book, hidden among the things in the chest. When you showed me what your father was wearing when he returned home, I saw the edges protruding among the clothes. A velvet binding and some edges of vellum.' I had an idea now what that book might be.

Margaret Walker would have protested again, but Lillis demanded the key and unlocked the chest. She tossed the concealing garments out on to the floor and turned towards me, the folio clutched between both hands. Her mother groaned in despair and covered her face with spread fingers. Lillis laid the book carefully on the table in front of me, then stood back to admire it, her head tilted a little to one side.

And indeed, it was still beautiful, even though the covers were rubbed and worn almost through in places, the gilt clasps and tassels badly tarnished, and many of the silk studs, which decorated the front, missing. The leaves were made of the finest vellum, and the script was most carefully done. I opened it at random and read a few lines from the Gospel according to Saint John. And although I had already guessed it to be a Lollard Bible, it nevertheless came as a shock to read the words in English instead of Latin; to have immediate understanding, rather than experience that delay necessary with translation. And the sayings of Our Lord sprang from the page marvellously fresh and vibrant, no sentence deleted at the discretion of a priest, no passage omitted because it was too contentious, or, more importantly, because it was ambiguous and might be understood two ways. I could see at once why the Church was so anxious to suppress the reading of the Scriptures in English, for every man and woman in the land could then make his or her own interpretations of Christ's word.

I kept these thoughts to myself, however, merely asking, 'How did Master Woodward come by this book?'

Margaret Walker uncovered her face, relieved, I think, that I had not recoiled in horror or threatened such heresy with exposure to the authorities. My smile must have encouraged her further, for she even managed one herself. 'I don't know,' she answered, 'but someone must have given it to him. It's a gentleman's book, as you can see. Father could never have afforded anything so beautiful himself.'

I nodded, sure that I knew the donor. 'Was Master Woodward able to read?' I asked.

'None of us can read,' Lillis put in, drawing up a stool beside mine. 'But I should like to learn my letters if someone would teach me.' She gave me a challenging stare.

'No, Father couldn't read,' Mistress Walker confirmed, 'but the preacher would read the book to him whenever he called.'

'He took it with him to Bell Lane?'

'Yes. I brought it back here when I thought him dead. I know I should have got rid of it, but I couldn't. I hid it in that chest, and I was glad, afterwards, that I did, for it gave him some peace and comfort in his dying days when his poor brain was addled from the beating he had taken.'

'And when he was really dead, you still could not bring yourself to dispose of it to one of your Lollard neighbours, such as Burl Hodge?'

Margaret immediately laid a finger to her lips and bade me hush. 'We know these things, but never mention them aloud.'

'You have never felt tempted by the heresy yourself?' I asked, and she shook her head vigorously.

'Let other fools jeopardize their lives. Indeed, I have

been unforgivably stupid to keep that book. I shall rid myself of it as soon as I can.'

Yet, with sudden insight, I knew that she wouldn't. In spite of the fact that it was a danger to her, she would go on concealing it at the bottom of the chest because it had meant so much to her father. It was in that moment that I first realized the strong, fierce loyalty both mother and daughter had for those they loved. On an impulse, I turned and took Lillis's hand. 'I'll teach you your letters,' I promised, 'when we have time.'

The blinding, joyous smile she gave me transformed her thin features, making her almost beautiful. I wondered how I could ever have thought her plain. Together, we replaced the Bible in the bottom of the chest, and started to pile the clothes on top. This time, the two women's dresses went in first, followed by the blanket, sheets and the old burel cloak. The shoes and hose came next, and finally the clothes worn by William Woodward. Lillis threw in the boots, and once again I noticed how they had been pushed out of shape because they had been crafted for a smaller person. But not that much smaller, or the seams of the drawers and shirt would have burst rather than being merely strained. I shook out the amber doublet once more, and it was then that I saw the faint, rust-coloured stains across the neck and shoulders.

Chapter Sixteen

I must have exclaimed aloud, because I suddenly realized that the two women were looking inquiringly at me.

'What is it?' Lillis asked, and when I held out the doublet, she came to peer over my shoulder and I could feel her soft breath against my cheek.

'Bloodstains. Look. These faint, rust-coloured marks around the neck. And see here! Others on the shoulders.'

Margaret reached across her daughter and took the garment from me, subjecting it to close inspection. 'You're right,' she nodded at last. 'The doublet's been washed and bleached in strong sunlight, but if you look carefully, you can still make out some of the stains. The velvet has lost its colour and is frayed in patches, as though it has been rubbed between two stones.'

Trembling with excitement, I pulled the shirt out of the chest and held it, in its turn, up to the light. At first I thought there was nothing to see, for linen, especially bleached linen, is easy to clean, and stains of any kind can be removed without much trouble. It was Lillis who thought of the rushlight, holding it so that its pale flame illuminated the material from the other side, to show me a faint tidemark of rusty-brown close to the neck-band.

'I – I don't understand,' Margaret faltered. 'These aren't the clothes Father was wearing when he was abducted. These are the ones he returned home in.'

I sat back on my haunches, frowning, while Lillis folded the doublet and shirt before restoring them to the chest. She closed the lid.

I said slowly, 'We're seeing things wrongly somehow. There must be a different way of looking at events which would help make sense of this discovery. Your father must have been attacked while he was wearing these clothes.' I suddenly remembered the mysterious horseman seen by Henry Dando, riding the bay. Why did I think that he might have been wearing the apparel now laid away in lavender and musk in Mistress Walker's oaken coffer? Henry Dando had not mentioned an amber doublet, it was true, but there was also a good frieze cloak, lined with squirrel's fur, and on a cold March morning this would undoubtedly have been worn, concealing what was under-neath. I had no proof or valid reason for this assumption of mine, but I felt in my bones that I was right. Maybe Henry Dando, without realizing it, had recognized the cloak as well as the horse, if he had seen Edward Here-path wearing it at some time.

'Did you ever show these things to anyone else?' I asked Margaret Walker. 'To Mistress Ford, for example?'

'Not to her, no. It was good of her to visit Father, but

she could only bear to stay a few minutes, and I did not wish to burden her with details. Master Herepath could not bring himself to come at all, but he did send soup from his kitchen. Although it was a bitter brew, undrinkable.'

I suspected another motive for Margaret's reticence, her fear that possession of such costly garments might be considered unlawful on her part and the true owner sought. She had plans, no doubt, to sell them if her fortunes ever became desperate, and I for one did not blame her.

'To anyone at all, then?' I persisted.

'Nick Brimble was the only person. It was he who advised me to say nothing and conceal them.'

I rose to my feet. 'You've committed no wrong that I can see. Someone gave these clothes to your father to wear, therefore they were his by law and now are yours.'

'I told you so, Mother.' Lillis smiled with mocking affection, then turned her attention back to me. 'But what does it all mean?'

I was unexpectedly moved by the trusting, childlike expression on her face; her confident belief that I would be able to explain. I felt as though I were betraying that trust when I shook my head. 'I'm afraid I can't give you an answer at the moment. Maybe I shall be able to find one when I've thought about things more carefully.'

'You need your supper,' Mistress Walker told me briskly. 'Lillis! Draw a mazer of ale from the barrel while I get some of the salted eels from the crock. They'll go well with the rest of the oatcakes left over from breakfast.'

As the two women fussed around me, both anxious for my comfort, I felt truly at home for the first time since my enforced stay with the Walkers, and began to think that, after all, I should do well to make the cottage my winter quarters. What was there for me in Wells? My parents were dead and it was long, anyway, since I had lived there. Boyhood friendships cool with absence, and I had no living kin. And if I was not allowed to sell within Bristol city walls, there were plenty of surrounding villages where I could ply my trade. Besides, if I married Lillis . . . I pulled myself up short. This was indeed running before I had learned to walk. I must give myself time to get used to the idea.

I spent a restless night, tossing and turning on my truckle bed, my mind shifting uneasily between my own problems and those of the mystery I had promised to solve. Eventually, however, personal worries sank beneath the greater complexities of William Woodward's disappearance. There was his bloodstained hat fished from the River Frome, and the bloodstained clothes in which he had returned home, five months after he had last been seen alive. Too much blood altogether. In the meantime, a man had been hanged for his murder, even though no body had been found, such had been the general conviction of Robert Herepath's guilt. Yet there was no doubt about the fact that Robert had stolen his brother's money, nor that he had been an unpleasant young man, wild and debt-ridden. Only one person had loved him, apart from his elder brother, and even she had turned against him at the last.

My straw-filled mattress seemed suddenly full of lumps, and I sat up with a silent curse. On the other side of the curtain, Margaret Walker was snoring, and Lillis, I guessed, was also asleep. She had seemed tired after supper, retiring early and giving me a shy, swift peck on the cheek. Happiness at my change of attitude towards her had made her sleepy, and I realized uneasily that she drew her strength from anger and aggression. All the same, I had given my word to teach her her letters, and that at least I would do before finally making a decision about marriage.

In the past, I had sometimes known inspiration to strike in the quiet of the early hours, but that night I was too confused to set my mind in order. There were thoughts just below the surface, like fish glimpsed beneath the ice of a frozen stream, but as yet I was unable to crack the ice to free them. I said my prayers again, repeating the familiar words and phrases to give myself comfort, but finally I added a plea of my own. 'Lord Saviour,' I said, not without a note of severity in my tone – for I have never believed that God demands grovelling sycophancy, whatever the Church might say – 'if you wish me to solve this mystery, you will have to give me a helping hand. It isn't fair to leave everything up to me.' I added a little petulantly: 'I haven't been well, remember!'

After that, I lay down once more, curled on to my right side, and was sound asleep within minutes.

I had finished breakfast and was sitting at the table, shaving. Lillis had gone to the dyer's to fetch more wool for her mother, and Mistress Walker herself was at the other end of the table, about to start the day's cooking. She was making black pudding, mixing oatmeal and fat and sheep's blood together in equal proportions. I paused to watch her for a moment or two before removing the last of my beard. I was putting my razor back in my pack when Lillis returned with the laden basket. She gave me her wide cat's grin.

'Black pudding,' she said. 'Good. My favourite.'

I pulled on my leather jerkin. 'I'm afraid I shan't be sharing it with you. I'm going away for a few days, to Gloucester.'

'Gloucester?' Margaret Walker looked up, dismayed. 'What do you want to go there for?'

'You've no horse,' Lillis objected.

'I don't need one,' I answered, 'while I've my own two legs. It will only take me two or three days. I know the road. I've walked it more than once. Thirty miles, perhaps, as the crow flies.'

'But why?' Mistress Walker insisted.

I debated for a moment whether or not to tell them, but could see no reason why they should not know. 'I want to find out if Edward Herepath really spent Thursday and Friday night in the city, as he said he did, last March; the night of the Annunciation of Our Lady and the following one. Maybe, even after all this time, someone will remember him.'

'But why should you doubt his word?' Lillis demanded.

'I need to find out if he was speaking the truth,' I

answered stubbornly. 'You asked me to unravel this mystery, and that is what I'm trying to do.'

She turned impetuously to Margaret for support. 'Tell him not to go, Mother! He's been ill. The weather's bad. He'll kill himself.'

'I doubt that. Not a great lad like him.' Mistress Walker eyed me levelly. 'Will you be coming back?'

I returned her glance, look for look. 'You have my promise.'

At that, she relaxed, and continued making her black pudding with renewed vigour. 'In that case, you must do as you see fit.' She wiped her hands on her apron. 'You'll need money. You've paid me well over the weeks. Let me return some to you.'

'No,' I said firmly. 'I have a little of my own store left, enough to start me on my way. I shall take my pack and sell as I go. I have been idle far too long.'

'It will delay you,' she argued. 'You will be gone longer than you need.'

'I have given my word to return.' I began fastening the pack on my back. 'You have no cause to be uneasy. But I need to feel the road beneath my feet again; to feel free and not bound by charity; to feel space all around me instead of being confined by city walls.'

I saw the sudden look of comprehension on Margaret Walker's face as she realized that I would never wholly settle down to a life of domesticity; that I was a rover by choice and not of necessity. I had of course told her and Lillis some of my past history, during the evenings when

191

we had been gathered round the fire together, but I think until that moment, she had not quite accepted that my decision to become a chapman had not, in some way or another, been forced on me by circumstances. It therefore came as a shock to her to discover that wanderlust was in my nature, at its very core.

'Even wanderers over the face of the earth need a place to return to,' I said quietly, arranging my cloak around myself and the pack, until I looked like a monstrous hunchback. I saw that she understood me, and guessed that she would come to terms with things as they were, not as she would like them to be. She was a practical woman who had learned not to expect too much of life. She wanted a husband for Lillis and grandchildren to dandle on her knee. She had also, I suspected, wanted the comfort of a man's constant presence in the cottage, for she had had to cope too long on her own; but if that was not God's will, she would settle for what she was offered.

Not so her daughter. Lillis threw herself at me and locked her thin arms about my neck. 'You shan't go! I forbid it!' she said fiercely.

I laughed as I looked down into the angry little face so close to mine, lips parted to reveal small, sharp teeth, eyes blazing with fury. I put up my hands and ruthlessly tore hers apart, freeing myself from her clasp. 'I'm going,' I said calmly, 'and neither you nor anyone else can stop me.'

'I will stop you! I will!' She beat with the full force of her strength against my chest. 'You're not to leave me!'

Margaret looked on, a cynical smile twisting her mouth, for she knew already who would win the battle. My strength and height have always given me an unfair advantage, and so it proved then. I simply picked Lillis up and put her to one side as I made for the door, leaving her sobbing with impotence.

Grinning, I went back and, tilting up her small pointed chin, planted a kiss firmly on her lips. They tasted faintly salty. 'You'll see me when you see me,' I told her, 'and not before. But you *will* see me.' I kissed her once more and then was gone.

I was free. I was on my own. I had escaped the petty tyrannies of the women. There was a spring in my step, in spite of the overcast morning, as I walked across the Frome Bridge and under the arch of Frome Gate into Lewin's Mead. This indeed had once been a meadow, belonging many years ago, or so I had been told, to one of the castle reeves; but dwellings had now encroached on the open space, including some of the outbuildings of the Franciscan friary. It was the fate, even then, of so much of our land, as towns began to spread outside their walls. And nowadays, of course, in this year of Our Lord 1522, towns are stretching their tentacles even further into the countryside, and I can foresee the time when walls will cease to be of any practical use. But everything changes, and I suppose it is only old men, like myself, who regret the past.

From Lewin's Mead I made my way through Silver

Street to Magdalen Lane, past the nunnery, which made me think at once of Cicely Ford. My heart lurched a little at the memory of her hand tucked into the crook of my arm and her sweet, gentle face turned confidingly up to mine. But I had seen God at work there; she was not for me nor for any man. I turned into Stony Hill, the path the mysterious horseman had travelled that March morning of last year, and, with St Michael's Church on my left, I climbed steadily in the direction of the windmill, perched on the high ground above the city. Its sails were turning in a freshening breeze, for there is always a wind blowing on the heights surrounding Bristol. I paused for a moment, looking back at the town, at the houses clustering, as they had for centuries, around the confluence of the Frome and the Avon. Then I set my face resolutely nor-nor-east, towards Gloucester.

By nightfall, I had reached only as far as the old Cheap town of Sodbury, where I was able to sell some of my wares in the market-place, and so buy myself a night's lodging at a respectable inn. The next day being Sunday, I attended both the services of Tierce-Sext and None before deciding to wait until the morrow before resuming my journey. I also attended Vespers at the parish church, much to the amusement of the landlord and his wife, who were well aware that my piety had much to do with their beautiful daughter, who was herself a model of religious devotion.

The next morning, however, early, I prised myself away, and with the family's good wishes ringing in my ears, as well as two of the landlady's chicken pasties nestling in my pocket, I took once more to the road. My boots were soon mired with filth from the uneven track, and a sudden flurry of sleet caused me to pull up my hood and wrap my cloak more securely about me. Everything was dank, gloomy and miserable; a passing horseman in a scarlet cloak was the only splash of colour in the landscape. There were far fewer people travelling in the depth of winter, all those who had no need to sensibly remaining mewed up at home by the fireside. And, as a carelessly driven cart splashed me to the thighs, discomforts I had borne for the past three winters without complaining suddenly seemed an unnecessary penance. Well, Margaret and Lillis Walker were waiting for me . . .

My journey, in the end, took five days, for I carried my pack into isolated hamlets and villages where the inhabitants were delighted to receive any traveller at that season of the year, and particularly one who was able to replenish the women's store of needles and thread, offer the men a new hunting-knife, and the young girls ribbons for their hair. I could have sold three or four times as much as I had in my pack, but my stock had been low when I set out, and I often cursed myself that I had not replenished it at Bristol dockside before leaving. But I suppose it would have delayed me even more and, as it was, on reaching Gloucester, my purse was as full as it would hold.

It was almost dusk on Thursday as I passed beneath the porch of the West Gate into the still busy street, where the bustle of the day's market was just beginning to wane. I stopped at a haberdasher's, where I bought a fresh pair of hose – the ones I was wearing being soaked through – and a jaunty russet hat which cost me sixpence; then at a pie-stall for my supper. The refilling of my pack, I decided, could wait for the moment, and I went in search of St Oswald's Priory, which I discovered in the shadow of the great cathedral church of St Peter. Here I slept on the floor of the guest hall, with several other travellers who were seeking a night's asylum from the elements, and awoke in the morning to a breakfast of dried fish and oatmeal, a reminder that Friday had come round again. As I doused my head under the pump and tried to hack the beard from my chin with a blunt razor, I thought of Lillis, of warm water and a knife-blade always carefully sharpened. I was missing her; I was missing my bodily comforts. To my amazement, freedom was beginning to pall a little. I was actually looking forward to going . . . yes, to going home.

Chapter Seventeen

Overnight, the rain had stopped and the sky cleared. It was one of those days when everything has an edge to it; the distant trees and roof-tops seemed carved from thunderclouds. Later on, it would rain again. I recognized the signs but, for the moment, sunlight glittered on a thin scattering of snow across the cobbles. The air was cold against my face and the windows of the houses I passed rattled in response to a rising breeze.

Following my instinct, I made my way straight to the inn close to St Peter's Abbey, built over a hundred years earlier to accommodate pilgrims visiting the murdered Edward II's tomb, but still known locally as the New Inn. And I was right to do so, for in the few minutes' conversation, obligingly spared me by the harassed landlord, I garnered much necessary information. Sweating profusely in his leather apron, his bald head shining in the early morning light, he was summoned by a pot-boy from the kitchens, where he was overseeing the cooking of breakfast for his numerous guests. In such circumstances, he might have been forgiven for a show of ill-temper, but he was one of those rare souls who have courtesy and patience for all their fellow men, be they of high or low degree.

'Last March,' he murmured, scratching his ear with a greasy forefinger. 'By the Virgin, that's a fair time ago, Master. The Day of the Annunciation ... Now, wait a minute! I do remember something. A biggish man, you say, this Master Herepath. A gentleman, well-dressed and riding a roan mare ... Yes, I have him. He arrived late in the evening, after the goodwife and I returned from Compline. We had been unable to go to church earlier, but would always wish, you understand, to pay devotion to Our Lady. He was heavily mired about the legs and feet, having come, he told us, from Bristol, riding throughout the day, and took our best bedchamber, together with a private parlour. Yes, yes! Of course I remember, now you jog my memory.'

'How long did he stay?'

The landlord considered my question, his head thoughtfully tilted to one side, and ignoring vociferous demands for his presence from the ale-room. He was quite content for the present to stand in the yard and give me all his attention.

'He stayed ... Yes, he remained two nights, the Thursday and the Friday. And it comes back to me that on the Friday morning he had a visitor, a man I know by sight who lives on the edge of town, close by the Grey Friars. They went off together somewhere, and then what happened? Let me see . . . Yes, I have it! Master Herepath returned leading a horse, a big, handsome black gelding with white stockings. He asked for extra stabling for the night, and the next day set out again for Bristol, riding the black and with the roan on a leading rein, tethered to his bridle.' The landlord broke off to call to a hurrying pot-boy: 'Tell the gentlemen I'm coming. I shan't be much longer.'

'And Master Herepath remained at the inn for the rest of the day?' I pressed, sensing that I was beginning to lose his interest.

'He certainly slept here,' the landlord conceded, 'but he was away and busy about his own pursuits for the hours of daylight. Indeed!' The ear was vigorously rubbed once more as animation returned. 'Now I think carefully, he arrived back at the inn some time after dark . . . and came in, I recall, with the ringing of the curfew bell!' The landlord was pardonably triumphant at these prodigies of recollection. 'He said he was the last man in at the West Gate before it was closed for the night. He had missed his supper, but my wife who, I have to admit, is susceptible to a handsome face, gave him soup and bread and cheese and ale in his room. And now, Master, you must excuse me. My guests are shouting for me, as you can hear. I trust I've been of some assistance to you.'

'You've been more than helpful, and I thank you. Just one more thing before you go. What was the name of the man from whom Master Herepath bought the gelding?'

The landlord paused in the open doorway of the ale-room, his honest brow furrowed. As the clamour from within grew too loud to be ignored any longer, he flung over his shoulder, 'Master Richard Shottery, if I remember rightly.'

This tallied with what Edward Herepath himself had told me, and I therefore set out with confidence for the Franciscan friary and the network of streets and alleyways surrounding it. A very few inquiries directed me to the home of Richard Shottery, a hatchet-faced, sharp-nosed man who was as reluctant to talk to me as the inn-keeper had been willing. Fortunately, I had left my pack behind at the priory, and so was able to disguise my true calling, for he would never have stooped to speak to so humble a person as a chapman. As it was, I was kept standing in his presence.

'You say you are a servant of Edward Herepath? Don't tell me there's anything wrong with the black I sold him, for I shan't believe you. As fine a piece of horseflesh as you're likely to find anywhere in the kingdom.'

'No, no,' I assured him hurriedly, 'my master is more than satisfied with the animal, but he is a man who likes to keep precise details of all his transactions. He is unsure of the day on which he bought the gelding from you, and as I was passing through Gloucester on his business, he commissioned me to approach you in this matter.' And God forgive me, I thought, for the lies I am telling. I prepared myself to do penance after my next confession.

Master Shottery snorted indignantly. 'And he sends you to trouble me on this paltry matter? It was last March. The day after Lady Day.'

'In the morning?'

'God's Nails, what does it matter? Morning, afternoon, evening . . . Yes, yes, in the morning, for he was very laggard in making up his mind and I was afraid I would have to ask him to stay to dinner. Not that I should have minded, you understand, but my wife was recovering from a sickness.' Richard Shottery glowered at me from beneath his thick eyebrows, plainly annoyed at finding himself on the defensive. 'Now, unless you have any other questions to ask me, I have business to attend to.'

I bowed obsequiously, as became a good servant, and took my leave, well-satisfied with this corroboration of the landlord's story. I returned to St Oswald's Priory where I collected my pack and then went in search of one of the brothers who might be at leisure. My first thought was for the infirmary, and here, indeed, I found several elderly monks recovering from winter ailments, either in bed or huddled together for warmth around the fire burning on the hearth. They willingly made room for a stranger in their midst, eager to exchange their small store of gossip for my larger one of the outside world. After a while, I was able to bring the talk round to the increasing spread of heresy among the poor, particularly that disseminated by the followers of Wycliffe, at which there was an instant hiss of indrawn breath and much shaking of venerable heads. Gloucester, it seemed, was nearly as big a hotbed of Lollardism as Bristol, and the pernicious evil was spreading westwards into Wales. Only last year, one of the brothers told me, his few remaining teeth clicking together in horror, three Lollards had been apprehended on the other side of the Severn, preaching their heretical message throughout the villages and hamlets of the forest, as they made their way through the marches which separate England and Wales.

'But others come to take their place,' he added with a sigh. 'It will need all our voices, Master Chapman, to overcome the Devil, so I exhort you to say your prayers.'

I promised him I would, feeling a little ashamed that I had misled the good brothers with my show of piety, for my beliefs were as confused then as they still are today, though I suppose, even now, I should claim to be a devout son of Holy Church. But am I? I can only hope that my Maker will understand better than I do myself, when I finally stand before Him on the great Day of Judgement. I shouldered my pack, said my adieus, and set off in the direction of the West Gate, stopping to buy three meat pies for my dinner from a pie-shop on the way. Once through the archway and past the gate-house, I walked until I reached the nearest crossing of the Severn.

By the time it reaches Gloucester, the Severn has narrowed, and there are several bridges which span its width. I chose the nearest crossing to the city, entering almost at once the outskirts of the forest which clothe the opposite banks. This is a strange, wild area, primeval trees enclosing an elemental and barbaric world, set apart from civilization. Tin is mined in the forest, and the small communities are a law unto themselves, holding their own courts and meting out far harsher penalties to offenders than any which the King at Westminster could devise. You can, as I discovered, ride for hours without seeing a soul, yet with the constant feeling that eyes are watching your every move. And when, at last, you do come face to face with one of the inhabitants, the men are frightening creatures, with blanched skin and stunted growth, like troglodytes sprung from the bowels of the earth to stare about them with blinking and hostile eyes.

It was late afternoon, and darkness was falling rapidly. I began to be afraid. I was alone and on foot, with only my cudgel for protection, hungry and lost. With what confidence I had marched into the forest a few hours earlier! Why had I not paused to think that I did not know my route? I had assumed that I should soon come upon habitations, that there would be other wayfarers beside myself, that the forest paths would bear the tracks of many feet, making them easy to follow between one village and another. But the Forest of Dean is not like that; you need a guide who knows its labyrinthine ways. I have been back once or twice in the years since then, but never again have I attempted to cross the forest on my own.

I began to suspect that I was going round in circles, for several trees I passed had a familiar look, particularly one large oak with a scar upon its trunk; but, search as I might, I could not discover the track by which I had entered the woodlands, and which passed between quiet homesteads clustered near the bridge. At last, shivering and icy cold, I wrapped myself in my cloak and curled up against the trunk of the oak, my stomach so empty that it hurt. I could hear small, nocturnal rustlings among the undergrowth, and the distant cry of a fox, up and hunting from its lair. I gripped my cudgel, taking a certain amount of comfort from the smooth feel of the wood in my palm. And the foliage above me was so dense that no rain could penetrate the leaves.

In spite of my discomfort, I must have fallen into an uneasy sleep, for I remember dreaming; a stupid, nonsensical dream, a jumble of the past week's events. After chasing me through the streets of Gloucester, the hooded man had just caught me by the shoulder, which he was vigorously shaking, when I came cleanly and suddenly awake. Someone was crouching over me, a small, bloodless face illuminated by the light from a lantern held in a thin, white hand. The voice which spoke in my ear was hoarse, as though speech was an art which my rescuer had not quite mastered.

'You're lost, Master.'

'Yes,' I agreed. 'I am.'

'You alone?' When I nodded, the man continued, 'You shouldn't be out on your own this time o' night, in the forest. You'd best come along with me. My woman'll feed ee and give ee shelter, if you don't mind lyin' in with the animals.'

'I've done it before now,' I answered gratefully, scrambling stiffly to my feet. My companion also straightened up, but came no higher than midway between my shoulder and my elbow. 'But you can't live near here. There are no dwellings anywhere about.'

The man laughed, a rusty, creaking sound. 'You're wrong there, Master.'

And I was, for we seemed to have been walking no time at all when I found myself in the centre of a circle of cottages. How we got there, I never knew, for it was now completely dark; and I speculated fruitlessly on how nearly I must have approached the settlement more than once that day, without being aware of its existence. My guide led me forward to one of the houses which, in the frail glow from his lantern, I could see were made of daub and wattle with turf roofs, smoke rising through holes in the middle. Inside, there was a beaten-earth floor, a central hearth, a bed of dried brushwood and animal pelts, a rough table, two three-legged stools, and a pig and a goat in a wooden pen. A small, half-naked girl and boy were already asleep beneath the pile of skins, and did not wake at our entry. A woman, as etiolated as her man, was kneeling beside the fire, stirring the contents of an iron pot, set among the burning logs.

She glanced up, her pale eyes widening in alarm as I towered above her. But she quickly got over her fright, getting to her feet and eyeing me suspiciously. 'Where did he come from?'

'Lost in the forest.' My host dragged forward one of the stools. 'Sit down, Master. Woman, he's cold and hungry. Give him to eat.'

His wife, or so I presumed her to be, fetched a wooden bowl from a stack on the table and ladled me out some stew. I have no idea what was in it – hare, perhaps, with herbs and vegetables – but it was the most delicious meal I have ever eaten. I was ravenous, it is true, but the flavour was unequalled by anything I have ever tasted either before or since. The woman watched silently while her husband and I ate our fill, replenishing my bowl as it emptied, until I was eventually forced to hold up a regretful hand. Only then did she get her own supper. Later, she made me a bed close to the animal pen, by taking more brushwood from a pile in the corner, and throwing on top of it one of the pelts which covered the sleeping children. Without a word, she and the man climbed in beside their offspring and, in moments, were sound asleep.

I went outside, relieved myself, then fell on my own bed fully clothed, expecting to lie awake for hours. But I was so tired that neither the smell of the goat nor the snortings of the pig could prevent me from being asleep within minutes.

A blast of icy air woke me, and I sat up on my pile of brushwood to see my friend of the night before re-entering the hut with a pail of water. It was still pitch-black outside, but there was a general atmosphere of bustle which told me it was morning. As I picked the twigs from my clothes and ran an exploratory hand across two days' growth of beard, my host poured the water into the iron pot and set about lighting the fire.

'Sleep well?' he grunted.

'Like the dead,' I assured him, conscious by now that I was being watched by two pairs of bright, excited eyes.

'Who is he, Father?' the girl wanted to know.

206

'Stranger, lost in the forest.' The man became aware of the child's semi-naked state and added roughly, 'Get thy smock on.' This was a garment of coarse, homespun linen, and when she had donned it, her father nodded in approval. To me, he said, 'Draw near the fire and warm yourself, Master. There's a pump outside if ee wants to wash.' He spoke as one who was conversant with the odder habits of strangers.

The woman had begun throwing oatmeal into the heating water, together with a handful of dried herbs, which hung in bunches from hooks driven into the wattle frame of the cottage. She was as silent as the night before, but the children, overcoming their shyness, had drawn close to me and, with the natural curiosity of their age, wanted to talk. But they waited until their father had once more gone outside.

'Where you from, Master?' the boy asked, wiping his hand across his running nose, then down the sleeve of his shirt, made from the same coarse homespun as his sister's shift.

'When I was a lad I lived with my mother in Wells,' I told him. 'But now I'm a chapman, and I wander from village to village peddling my wares. So you could say I don't belong anywhere nowadays.' I thought of Lillis and Margaret Walker and felt as though I had betrayed them. 'Do you get many strangers here? People like myself, lost in the forest?'

'Sometimes,' the girl admitted. 'But most people hire a guide. My father and the rest of the miners here will show you the way if you pay them.'

Her brother added, plainly bursting with importance, and pleased to show off in front of the stranger, 'We have a horse now.' Ignoring his mother's warning cry of 'Hamo!' he continued, 'Leastaways, the head man o' the village keeps it tethered behind his cottage, but 'tis for everyone's use if they need it.'

My heart beat faster in excitement. 'What sort of horse?' I asked. 'What colour?'

'Who's talking o' horses?' The man had returned with an armful of twigs and branches, and he stood in the doorway, glaring balefully at his son.

The woman looked fearful, rising from her crouching position by the fire, ready, if necessary, to step between husband and child. 'Leave him be, man,' she said quietly. 'He's said naught amiss.'

'What goes on in this village is our business,' her husband retorted angrily, 'and not for the ears of strangers.'

I rose slowly to my feet. Loath as I was to get young Hamo into further trouble, I could not let the subject drop.

'This horse,' I said, 'I'd like to see it.' I flung up a hand as if to blind myself to my host's fierce gaze. 'I promise I won't attempt to take it from you or bring trouble upon the community, but it is very important that I take a look at it. Is it a light bay with black points and a white snip between its nostrils?'

There was a deathly silence for a moment, then the woman gave a moan. 'I always knew we were doing wrong, keeping that animal.'

Chapter Eighteen

The man said fiercely, 'Hold thy wist!' and he included his son in his furious glare. 'Thee both need tongue-locking!' He dropped his bale of faggots and raised a hand as if to hit whichever one was nearest. I stepped forward quickly and seized his wrist.

'Don't blame your woman and son, for I should have found out sooner or later. The reason I'm in the forest, the reason I'm travelling into Wales, is to seek information of a man named William Woodward, the grandfather of my affianced bride.' The words had slipped out before I was even conscious of them, and I realized suddenly that somewhere, somehow, I had made up my mind. For good or ill, I was committed to Lillis Walker and intended to make her my wife. 'From what I've heard, it seems I need go no further. I suspect he was found here, in the forest, last year, a day, maybe two, after the Annunciation of Our Lady. Am I right?'

The man, who had surprising strength for one so small and puny-looking, tore his wrist free of my grasp and backed away, his mouth set in a thin, hard line, prepared to maintain silence; but he had reckoned without the agitation of his wife. She was openly sobbing now, and her thin fingers clung to my arm.

'I do admit 'twas one of our number found him, but 'twasn't no one here who gave him the beating. It were Gwyn Gwynson stumbled across him and brought the poor gentleman to the village, and we women nursed him back to health. But we never knew his name nor where he came from, for his mind had gone from the blows he had got to his head. Kept repeating he'd been captured by Irish slavers, and that's all he would ever say. Master, you mun believe me, for 'tis God's truth.'

Accepting that the cat was out of the bag and that there was no getting it in again, my host said defensively, 'We didn't steal the horse. One of us found him wandering loose in the forest some days later, still saddled and bridled, but half-starved, poor beast. We meant to return him to the man you say's your woman's grandfather, but one day, he just up and left when nobody was about. Vanished into thin air. High summer it were by that time. He'd been with us three or four moons. There was a meeting o' the village elders, and the headman thought we mun keep the horse. God's Providence, he said it were, for sometimes 'tis needful to go quickly between one community and another. When one of our children is sick, and our Goody has no sovereign remedy, we can send to a neighbouring mine-head, and maybe their woman will have the answer. In such cases, 'tis a godsend to travel swift. If you take it from us, 'twill be an ill-service you do.'

'I have no intention of taking the horse from you,' I assured him. 'I just wish to see it, to be certain that it is the one that was lost.' Although I was already sure in my own mind that the animal was the one stolen from Master Herepath's stables. 'Can you take me now to the headman's cottage?'

But, as I spoke, a great clatter started up outside, two pieces of wood being loudly banged together. I guessed it to be the signal for the men to go to the mine-shaft and be lowered in their cage. It was time for the day's work to begin.

'And you with nothing in your belly!' the woman cried in alarm.

Her husband scornfully bade her hold her tongue. 'Give me a crust of bread to put in my pocket. That's all I need.' He eyed me up and down. 'If you'll be content to wait here, Master, until I return this evening, I'll take you to see the headman myself, and we'll hear what he's to say. If he thinks you trustworthy, and believes your story, he'll show you the animal. If not, he'll send you on your way no wiser. And don't think to be bringing the law down about our ears, for the sheriff's men, they won't meddle with the likes of us.'

That I could well understand.

I spent the day, from dawn to dusk, curled up by the fire, sometimes dozing, but more often just sitting quietly, piecing together the bits of knowledge which I'd gleaned over the past few weeks until they made a clear, whole picture in my mind. I thought now that I knew what had happened, the sequence of events and the motive behind them. Hamo and his sister, whose name was Gwynne, played in the dirt with the crude toys which, I guessed, they had fashioned themselves from odds and ends of rubbish which came to hand. And after a dinner of the stew which we had eaten yesterday, the woman, who had been busy all morning, sat with us near the fire and was prevailed upon by the children to tell stories of her grandfather, who had been recruited, along with many of his fellow miners, by the great Harry of Monmouth, to go to France and burrow beneath the walls of Harfleur. Weird and wonderful tales of foreign parts he had brought back to the forest when his job was done.

'I shall go beyond seas when I grow up,' Hamo declared stoutly.

'You'll go down the mine, like Father,' his sister told him, putting him in his place.

'I shan't! I shan't!'

'You will! You will!'

And they rolled over and over together on the floor, like two young puppies which snarl and scratch, but do not intend to hurt. Outside, the greyness barely lightened all day, so close-set and profuse were the surrounding trees. Dark, dripping and melancholic, they stood like sentinels on guard about the village, cutting it off from the rest of the world. I wondered if the sun ever penetrated the gloom. The sense of isolation was profound.

It was dark again before the man returned home, tired

and filthy after hours underground. But once he had eaten – bread and salted bacon with a mush of lentils – and held his head beneath the pump, he was ready to keep his promise and conduct me to the headman's cottage. He lifted down the lantern and lit the rushlight inside. Then, with a jerk of his head, he led me outdoors.

The headman's dwelling was set a little apart from the others with a paling around it, so giving it its own small plot of ground. Other than that, however, it was the same daub and wattle building with a turf roof as the rest of them, although inside, it did boast a proper bed with faded and much-mended tapestry curtains. The chief himself was not some old man, hoary with age, as I had half-expected, but one very much like the others I had glimpsed, of the same indeterminate number of years. It was difficult to reckon with any accuracy how many nativities each miner had celebrated, for their calling seemed to rob them of blood; their faces were lined, their bodies stooped from long hours bent almost double hewing at the seams of tin beneath the forest floor. As the father of two young children, I doubted if my host and rescuer could be more than twenty-five summers at the most, and probably not so much, but in appearance he could have been twice my age. The headman, on the other hand, looked just as old, or just as young, depending on how one viewed the matter.

Looking back, I realize that what impresses itself on me now, after this long period of time, is with what courtesy and patience these people received me. The sort of life they led might well have brutalized them, until they were no better than the wild beasts inhabiting the forest. But the strict discipline of the mining communities had prevented that from happening, and I only wish I had appreciated it more then. I was young, however, and too absorbed in my own affairs to waste consideration on the hardships of others less fortunate than myself.

My host, whose name I realized I still did not know, explained my request to the headman, who regarded me thoughtfully for a while without saying anything. Finally, he asked, 'You swear you do not wish to take the horse away? Nor report our possession of the animal to the Gloucester sheriff? We need not fear him and his *posse* disturbing the peace of the forest, searching for the beast to confiscate it?'

'I swear,' I answered. 'By Our Lady and all the Saints.'

The headman nodded, satisfied, heaving himself up from the stool on which he had been seated. 'I have to be certain, you understand, for it is a valuable animal. It would grace the stable of any nobleman, and would be worth the getting.' He indicated to my host that he should lead the way out of doors with his lantern. 'You have the light, Hamar, to guide us.'

Hamo, Hamar, Gwynne, Gwyn Gwynson; as I followed Hamar, I thought how alike names in the community seemed to be, and guessed that they had been used and re-used for many hundreds of years, reflecting those of the earliest miners in the settlement. It was no doubt the same all over the forest and, by his name, a man could easily be linked to a particular mining village. The evening air struck chill, for I was not wearing my cloak, and the grass was slimy and treacherous underfoot. I wondered how a piece of prime bloodstock, used to the comforts of the Herepath stables, had adapted to life in these primitive surroundings. But the bay, when I saw him, seemed perfectly content, and gave a whinny of pleasure when the headman caressed him. A stable had been built among the trees, of the same daub and wattle as the cottages, but with a far sounder roof of pitch, and straw liberally scattered over the floor, ankle-deep to keep his feet warm. A wooden manger, full of hay, and a wooden trough, filled with fresh spring water, supplied the animal's needs, while several layers of dry sacking were tied across his back and under his belly for warmth against the winter's chill. His eye was bright, his coat shining: he was happy and well looked after.

I had no doubt it was Edward Herepath's missing horse, for it was indeed light bay in colour, with black points and a white snip between its nostrils. It had been ridden here by William Woodward and cared for as his property; until one day, like an animal crawling back to die in its lair, his homing instinct had impelled him to quit the village on foot, to walk the long, dusty miles to Bristol. His poor, bewildered mind had forgotten everything after a certain moment, and he only remembered what he had to say when he finally returned home; that he had been captured by slavers and taken to Ireland. And as a child will do, repeating a lesson too well-learned, he had stuck to his story.

'You recognize the animal?' the headman asked me.

I had almost forgotten the presence of the others, so deeply had I been immersed in my own thoughts, and at the sound of his voice, I jumped. 'Y-yes, I think so,' I stuttered. 'I only know the beast by report, but I am sure it is the same one. Thank you for letting me see him. I shall trouble you no further.'

'Is there any other way in which we can serve you?' the headman inquired.

I answered eagerly. 'Is it possible to have words with Gwyn Gwynson who, I understand, discovered William Woodward in the forest?'

The headman nodded. 'You understand aright. It was Gwyn and his woman who nursed the stranger back to health, although his mind, alas, never recovered. Hamar will conduct you to his cottage. Hamar, tell Gwyn he has my leave to speak.'

I thanked him, and followed my host across the circle of grass to a dwelling almost directly opposite his own. Inside, it might have been Hamar's cottage, with the one exception that instead of two small children there were four – three boys and a girl – all somewhat older in years than Hamo and Gwynne. As we entered, there was the same strong odour blended of pig and goat, the acrid smell of smoke and human sweat. The family had finished eating and were seated huddled round the dying fire, warming themselves before crawling into bed. At the sight of Hamar and a stranger in their midst, their eyes brightened with interest; and when it was known what was wanted, together with the headman's permission to speak, the air became charged with excitement. Such a diversion would have been welcome at any time, but in the depth of winter it was doubly so.

A place was made for Hamar and me by the fire, some fresh branches of wood thrown on to revive the flames, and Gwyn's woman poured us each a cup of ale brewed from germander, bitter and dark. Only then, when hospitality had been offered and received, did Gwyn begin his story and tell me what I wanted to know.

It had been last year, he said, in early spring, the day following that of the Annunciation of Our Lady, that he had stumbled across a badly injured man some little way into the forest. 'He would have died, Master, if I hadn't found 'im, for he'd been beaten savagely about the head.'

'A mass o' blood there were,' the woman confirmed, 'all down his neck and over his shoulders. I thought at first 'is clothes were ruined, but I managed to clean 'em somehow, though it took a while.'

Her husband was turning on her to stem this interruption, when I asked quickly, 'What were his clothes like? Of what quality?'

'Oh, a gentleman's quality, no doubt o' that. 'Twas what made them so difficult to put to rights.'

'Can you describe them? The colour, the cloth.'

'Velvet, the doublet was, and fine wool the hose. And the cloak was lined with fur. As to the colour, the cape and hood were lined with scarlet, that I do remember, and the doublet a rich, deep yellow.'

'And you say you managed to get the bloodstains out?

217

A difficult task, I've always understood. How did you do it?'

The woman shrugged. 'Oh, aye, blood's not easy to wash away if the marks are set and old. But these were still fresh when my man brought the stranger home. I soaked 'em straight in water from the barrel.'

Her husband broke in here, plainly incensed at being excluded from the conversation for such a length of time, and anxious to reclaim my attention. ''E couldn't long've been attacked when I found 'im. The blood 'adn't even dried. A moment or so earlier, and I might've seen who did it. But if I'd found 'im much later, 'e'd've surely died.'

'What would have happened if he had?'

It was the man's turn to shrug. 'The animals of the forest would've got 'im. They say there's no wolves in these parts any more, nor've there been for hundreds of years. But I say I've seen 'em slinkin' in and out the trees.' The woman nodded solemnly in agreement, as did Hamar. Gwyn Gwynson went on: 'An' I've seen corpses what've been gnawed to the bone. You can't tell I that's not the work o' wolves.'

I asked, 'If the stranger had been killed and his body found by someone in authority, would the sheriff have pursued the matter?' My words were met with a blank stare. 'Would the sheriff have sent men to ask questions about the death?'

All three adults shook their heads. Hamar explained, 'There are footpads and thieves in the forest. Such deaths are too common to waste much time on.'

'So! If Gwyn here had not stumbled across my woman's grandfather – ' how strange those words sounded to my ears – 'he would have vanished without trace?'

''Tis possible,' Hamar confirmed.

'For there were nothing on him to tell us who he might be,' added Gwyn. He inquired eagerly: ''E got 'ome, then, the old man? Did 'e 'ave any notion where 'e'd been?'

I nodded, and shook my head almost simultaneously. 'Yes, he got home, but he always insisted he'd been captured by slavers and taken to Ireland.'

''E were babblin' of that when 'e were 'ere. Does it make any sense to you, Master?'

'Perhaps,' I answered, unwilling to commit myself and provoke further questioning. I changed the subject. 'Is there much heresy, here in the forest?'

I had been deliberately abrupt, hoping to shock my audience into some kind of admission, even if it were only by the expressions on their faces. In this I was successful, for although they all vigorously denied it, as I had guessed they would, I saw the fleeting glances of alarm which passed between them. I tried to make light of the matter. 'I only ask, because a man in Gloucester told me that, last year, three Lollard preachers had been apprehended this side of the Severn. And many more, he thought, had remained uncaught. The heresy, it seems, is taking root in Wales.'

'We don't meddle in other people's business,' Hamar told me shortly, and rose to his feet, indicating that I should do the same. Our visit was over, and it was I who

219

had brought it to a close by my interest in something which did not concern me. I had broken their golden rule that curiosity was the unforgivable sin. As long as I confined my inquiries to a subject which did concern me, because it pertained to my woman, they would afford me every courtesy and answer my questions to the best of their ability; but once I touched on so personal a matter as the religious beliefs of any of their number, then they saw no reason to humour me further. Good-nights were exchanged and my thanks coldly received by Gwyn and his family, but although I was sad at having to take my leave on such a sour note, I nevertheless could not regret my action, for I had gained my answer. I followed Hamar back to his cottage and rolled into bed, knowing that he would expect my departure first thing on the morrow, as soon as it was light.

Chapter Nineteen

My homeward journey took me only two days, for I had not refilled my pack and therefore had nothing to sell and no diversions to make. The day I left the miners' settlement was a Sunday, and I might, I suppose, have returned to St Oswald's Priory and waited there until the following day to make my purchases in Gloucester docks and market. But I had only one thought in mind by that time; to get home to Bristol as fast as I could and confront the person who had tried to murder William Woodward. And there was also a certain excitement at the prospect of seeing Lillis again; an excitement which, four weeks ago, I would not have allowed to be possible.

I spent my second night on the road in the hayloft of a farm, and by rising while it was still dark and pushing southwards with my longest stride, I saw the walls of Bristol below me by mid-morning. I passed beneath the Frome Gate to find the town in a bustle and a holiday air pervading the streets. It was only then, to my shame, I remembered that it was Candlemas, the Day of the

Purification of Our Lady, when Christ was presented by her to the elders in the temple. On this second day of February, the mayor and all the members of the City Guilds would walk in procession through the streets with their lighted candles. The great houses would be decorated with tapestries and streamers and all would be gladness and light.

But the Lollards would keep away on some pretext or another; those who worshipped secretly would plead illness, no doubt, or the illness of a child; for what other excuse would be deemed sufficient? I guessed that there would be a lot of sickness this day amongst the weavers of Redcliffe, for Lollards did not believe in the symbolic representation by candleshine of Our Lord as the Light of the World, or the Light to Enlighten the Gentiles. And, as I made my way beneath St John's Arch and up Broad Street, I recalled guiltily having once given ear to a man who told me that Candlemas was nothing more than the old Roman custom of burning candles to the pagan goddess Februa, the mother of Mars, to ward off evil spirits. Furtively, I crossed myself and hurried on.

At the top of Broad Street, however, I paused, suddenly recalling something Margaret Walker had said, turned to my right and then to my right again, which brought me into the narrow alley behind the Small Street houses. I walked slowly along its length until I was almost in Bell Lane. At the third gate from the end, I stopped and, lifting the latch, stepped softly into Edward Herepath's garden.

Fortunately there was no one about, and I was able to look around me. I regarded the small stone outbuilding thoughtfully, but then let my gaze roam over the rest of the plot. Eventually I found what I was seeking, but had not hoped to find. Indeed, I had not expected to discover anything at all; but there, in a corner, no doubt seeded from the great marsh, was a cluster of tall, purple-spotted stems, which in summer would blossom with white flowers.

As quietly as I had entered, I withdrew, closing the gate carefully behind me. My sense of elation grew with this seeming confirmation of yet another of my suspicions. As I proceeded on my way, I was cheered even further by the cessation of normal work and the festive preparations going on everywhere around me. People were in holiday mood and, in spite of the chill and miserable weather, called friendly greetings from almost every corner. Even across the bridge, there was a feeling of expectation. Spinning-wheels and looms were silent.

I entered Margaret Walker's cottage with a sense of arriving home. Nothing had changed, and I felt as though I had never been absent. Margaret was stirring the contents of a pot simmering over the fire, and there was a loaf of hot bread on the table, just brought fresh from the baker's oven by Lillis who, still wearing her cloak, was struggling to remove her pattens. Both women looked towards the door as I came in, and there was a moment's disbelieving silence. Then Lillis gave a cry and threw herself into my arms.

'You have come back!' she exclaimed, clinging to me fiercely and sobbing.

'I promised I would,' I answered. 'Didn't you trust my word?'

'We didn't know what to think.' Margaret spoke sombrely, and there was a note of accusation in her voice which made me regard her questioningly. 'Lillis,' she said 'is with child.'

Lillis lifted her head from my chest. 'Mother!' she protested. 'Not now.'

'He has to know sometime,' Margaret answered implacably. 'The sooner the better.' Her eyes met mine. 'You'll have to marry her. I'll not have folk round here calling her a wanton.'

'I've come back to do so,' I said, 'although I didn't know about the child.' Yet even as I spoke, I was aware of a sinking of the heart and a depression of the spirit. It is one thing to do something of your own free will, but from a sense of duty it is quite another. The old feeling of being trapped returned to haunt me. I pecked Lillis's cheek, ignoring her cries of rapture at my declaration.

Her mother's stern features relaxed, and she heaved a great sigh of relief. 'I'm glad to hear you say so, lad. Sit down, sit down. You must be tired after your journey. Eat first and tell us your adventures after.' She began ladling stew into a bowl. 'Did you find out what you hoped to?'

I shed my cloak and put my cudgel and pack in their usual corner. It struck me that I was indeed at home here now, and beginning to form domestic habits. The walls seemed to step a little closer, but I answered all their questions as cheerfully as I could, interspersing them with many of my own concerning Lillis's health. She appeared to be thriving, and it had only needed my return, Margaret said, for her to achieve perfect contentment. I had no doubt this was true, and tried hard to reconcile myself to the change of circumstances. After our meal, and when the pots had been washed and cleared away, we sat around the fire, talking. Lillis, uninterested in anything else, wanted to make plans for our marriage, but Margaret, satisfied now as to my intentions, was happy enough to want to listen to stories of my travels, and curious enough to want to know what I had discovered, if anything, about her father.

'Are you any wiser?' she asked me, and I nodded.

'I know where he was and I think I know why he was there. I also think I know who sent him, and why his life was attempted.'

Margaret Walker thought about this for a moment, then nodded. 'Someone tried to kill Father? Yes, I think perhaps, deep down, I have always suspected that. The beating had plainly been severe, more than a footpad would administer to steal a few trinkets, and certainly more than Irish slavers would mete out if they wished to sell their victim for a reasonable price. You are saying that he was left for dead?' Her interest sharpened suddenly as she realized that I had indeed made some discoveries worth the telling. She continued eagerly, 'You went to Gloucester to find out if Master Herepath was there when he claimed to be. Was he?'

'Oh, yes,' I said. 'So, if you'll listen a while, I'll tell

you all I know and all I think I know. But answer me one thing first. You told me that Cicely Ford brought broth to your father when she visited him, after his return. Did he drink it?'

Lillis cut in scornfully: 'The first time he did. But after that, he complained of it tasting bitter. And so it was. You'd think a man of Edward Herepath's wealth could afford a better cook. Why, even I could make a tastier broth than that!'

I felt that the 'even I' boded ill for my stomach's future well-being, and trusted that Margaret would continue to preside over the cooking-pots when Lillis and I were married.

Margaret hushed her daughter, no doubt reading my thoughts aright, and said quickly, 'There was something wrong with the soup. Tainted meat had been used. The cook probably had instructions not to use the best ingredients, for it was only out of the kindness of Mistress Cicely's heart that she brought us anything. After all, neither she nor Master Herepath had cause to love my father, however little he could be blamed for what had happened.'

I shook my head. 'It wasn't bad meat nor even bad broth, and the cook was innocent of one of the contents. Now, listen to me, both of you, and I'll tell you what I think really became of Master Woodward.'

It was well after noon when I finally quit the cottage, leaving behind me a dazed and shaken Margaret Walker, who still refused to believe the truth of what I had told her. Lillis had been easier to convince for, in spite of her childishness in some things, she was readier to accept that there was an evil side to human nature than her mother. She understood the baser emotions of greed and hate and envy because she was a prey to them herself, and therefore did not doubt that they existed also in other people.

As I made my way back to the centre of the town, candles were being lit, processions beginning to form, as Guild members and others assembled to worship at the various churches: the weavers at that of their patron saint – Catherine – in Temple Street; the kalendaries, who tend the sick, provide masses for the dead, and keep the charitable records of a city, at All Hallows; the rich merchants at St Ewen's. But there was one man of wealth and substance who, I suspected, would stay at home if he possibly could, to preserve himself from those 'splendid buildings and gaudy decorations' which, Wycliffe had maintained, 'drew away the mind of the worshipper'.

On this occasion, I approached Edward Herepath's house from the front, and was rewarded by the sight of Cicely Ford and Dame Freda just emerging into Small Street as I turned the corner. Each woman held a lighted candle and a missal.

'Master Chapman.' Cicely gave me her sweet, sad smile. 'Which church are you hurrying away to? Come with us to St Ewen's,' she added, ignoring, as always, her companion's scandalized protest.

'I'm afraid I cannot,' I said, bowing gallantly and recollecting how, a few weeks earlier, such an invitation would have made my heart sing. 'I have business to attend to. Master Herepath does not go with you?'

'No. He is unwell. Something he has eaten, I fear, has disagreed with him.'

'Nor Master Avenel?' I suggested with a faint lifting of my eyebrows.

She laughed. 'He would have escorted us, but I refused his offer.' Dame Freda snorted and Cicely turned towards her. 'Dear ma'am, I know you find me unreasonable in this, but believe me it's for the best. It would be most unfair to Robin to encourage him.'

The older woman looked as though she would burst into tears. 'Sweeting, if only you would rid yourself of this foolish notion of entering a religious order! I can only trust that when Master Herepath knows what you are about, he will forbid it.'

Cicely sighed. 'Poor Edward. It will hit him hard, I know. But he will not change my mind. Master Chapman, adieu. We shall be late if we do not hurry.'

I watched them go, continuing slowly in the opposite direction, until they had turned into Corn Street and disappeared from view. Then I retraced my steps to Edward Herepath's door and knocked for admittance. My first summons was ignored, so I knocked again, this time with greater urgency. After yet another delay, the latch was raised and Edward Herepath himself stood on the threshold. This did not altogether surprise me, for I had guessed that the servants would have been given leave to attend church and take part in the processions.

He stared at me in astonishment. 'What do you want?'

he demanded angrily. 'There is nothing further we have to say to one another.'

He started to close the door, but I put my foot between the jamb and the leaf. 'There is much we have to say, Master Herepath, believe me. Have you never wondered what happened to William Woodward during those months that he was missing? Well, I can tell you.'

I saw his hand tremble on the latch. His face, healthy looking enough before, in spite of his reported sickness, was now drained of colour, his eyes narrowed, half in disbelief, half in fear that I meant what I said. Would he take a risk and dismiss me with contempt? Or would his natural curiosity to discover how much I really knew get the better of him? After a moment, he held the door wide and bade me enter.

I followed him across the hall, with its rich reds and greens and blues, into the parlour beyond, where the green velvet cushions on the window-seat glowed in the fire-light, and the polished lid of the spruce coffer reflected the flames of candles in the holder of latten tin. All was as snug as I remembered it from my previous visit.

Edward Herepath cast himself down in the armchair but did not invite me to sit. 'Now,' he snapped, 'what is this nonsense? You weary me, so make it brief.'

'Very well,' I said. 'You killed your brother as surely as if you had strangled him yourself, by arranging the disappearance of William Woodward in circumstances which made it seem that he had been murdered. Is that brief enough?'

He looked at me as though I had taken leave of my

senses, then threw back his head and laughed. 'Get out of my house,' he commanded, 'before I have you thrown in prison!'

He was a good actor, and I might have been convinced had I not noticed the nervous twitch at the corner of his mouth. Deep down he was frightened, and was unable completely to conceal the fact. I stood my ground.

'You also attempted the life of William Woodward,' I went on, 'but failed. You left him for dead, but he was found in time by a tin miner from the forest, who took him home and nursed him back to health. Or as much health as was left to him. His mind never recovered, but you couldn't have known a moment's peace during those few months of life remaining to him, in case he suddenly recovered his wits and told the truth.'

'What truth?' Edward Herepath sneered. 'He told the sheriff's officers that he had been abducted by slavers and taken to Ireland, from where he had eventually escaped. Many doubted the story, I know, but I saw no reason to. Meanwhile, my poor unfortunate brother had been hanged for a murder he had not done, though, as Heaven's my witness, no one could be blamed for disbelieving his protestations of innocence. The money – the rents and debts collected on Lady Day by William – was in his possession, and one of the pouches containing it was bloodstained, as was the breast of his jerkin. Furthermore, several days later, William's hat, also bloodstained, was fished out of the Frome.' The sneer became more pronounced. 'Are you claiming that William arranged all these things himself?'

'With your help and guidance, yes. Oh, you couldn't force your brother to steal the money, that I admit. It was the one risk you had to run in your otherwise carefully laid plan. But given Robert's character, the fact that he was wild and constantly in debt, it was a very small risk. Mistress Walker told me that you admitted to informing your brother that William was to hold the money for you until your return from Gloucester.' It was I who laughed this time. 'You carefully make an arrangement with your rent collector, the whole purpose of which is to ensure that Robert and the money are not under the same roof during your absence, and then you let the information slip? That made me suspicious of you from the very first. It would have been the action of an incompetent fool, and that you most certainly are not.'

Edward Herepath came to his feet with a sudden movement which was surprisingly lithe in so heavily built a man. I was not expecting it and, caught off-guard, lost my balance and fell to the floor, pinned down beneath his weight. His hands found my throat while I was still struggling to free my arms, and had begun to tighten their grip when I managed, using all my strength, to throw him off. Before I could scramble to my feet, however, he was at me again, his murderous intent plainly written on his face. He had had time to reflect that I knew too much, that I had at least one witness to William Woodward's being in the neighbourhood of Gloucester when Edward himself was known to have been staying there; sufficient to plant the seeds of doubt in people's minds. I could not be allowed to tell my story, and my death was the only way to stop me. He had, as I well knew, a subtler, surer means of death at his command, but it would not serve his purpose. It had to seem that he had killed me while defending himself, and with only the two of us in the house, he could make up whatever story he pleased to satisfy the sheriff.

The murderous hands were almost at my throat again, but now I was ready and rolled beyond his reach. At the same time, I grabbed the top of the coffer and hauled myself to my feet. Edward Herepath was swiftly up as well and swung his fist in a well-aimed blow at my jaw. Fortunately I saw it coming, and jerked my head back so that it merely grazed my chin. He lost his balance, clutched at me for support and, a moment later, we were once more on the floor, locked in a lover-like embrace.

Had he been wearing a knife, he would not have scrupled to use it, and it was my good fortune that there was no such weapon to hand. He was a strong man; not so strong as I was when in the best of health, but my strength had been sapped by my illness, and by undertaking my recent journey before I was really well. And he had the advantage that, if he murdered me, he could explain the killing, whereas my salvation rested on keeping him alive.

As I felt my limbs begin to turn to water, I was filled with panic. My senses were swimming and my body was running with sweat. My adversary scented victory and, with a last great effort, he managed to get on top of me and plant one knee on my chest. I clutched desperately at his wrists, but his splayed hands fought their way nearer and nearer to my throat. In another minute, his thumbs would gouge at my windpipe . . .

The door opened, although neither Edward Herepath nor I was aware of it until a horrified voice exclaimed, 'Stop it! Stop it! Whatever is going on here? Both of you, get up!'

Chapter Twenty

Edward Herepath's arms went limp; the spread fingers relaxed and, with one heave, I dislodged him, scrambling to my feet. I saw his eyes widen with horror at the sight of Cicely Ford, standing in the doorway. Leaning against the coffer, I drew several deep breaths in order to clear my head.

The girl closed the parlour door behind her and advanced into the room. She was still clutching her missal, but had rid herself of the candle. She looked pale but composed.

'I was correct, then,' she said. 'I had this unaccountable feeling that something was wrong. I could not explain it, either to Dame Freda or to myself, and tried to shake it off. But at the very door of St Ewen's, I had to turn back and come home. Edward, what has happened? And Master Chapman, what are you doing here? When we met earlier, you did not say that you had business with my guardian.'

Edward Herepath had by now got up from the floor,

and he sank once more into his chair. He was sweating, his skin grey with fear, but he was not yet ready to admit defeat. He gave an unpleasant laugh. 'You may well ask the pedlar what he is doing here! He has come with some pernicious story, accusing me of murdering my own brother.'

'Robert?' Cicely's breath caught in her throat as she uttered the name. 'How could you? He was . . . he was . . . hanged.' She repeated, 'Hanged,' as though facing up to the word and all its implications for the very first time.

Her guardian nodded. 'And so the chapman knows full well. You may judge for yourself why I lost my temper, and so far forgot myself as to attack him.'

Cicely Ford turned towards me, her delicate oval features rigid with anger. 'What have you to say for yourself, Master Chapman?' She added reproachfully, 'I thought you my friend.'

'And so I am,' I answered levelly. 'I am also a friend to the truth, and I repeat that Master Herepath here killed his brother as surely as if he had set the noose about his neck with his own two hands. He also tried to murder William Woodward.'

'That's a foolish lie!' Her scorn was palpable. 'Edward was in Gloucester when William was abducted.'

'But Master Woodward was not abducted,' I said. Now that I was no longer in danger of violence from Edward Herepath – for he would hardly dare attack me in front of his ward – I felt myself to be once more in command of the situation. When Cicely Ford started to protest at this statement, I interrupted. 'If you would be willing to sit down and listen to me, you may judge my story for yourself.'

Edward Herepath stood up. 'I have had enough of this nonsense!' he exclaimed furiously. 'Neither Mistress Ford nor I wish to hear your lies. Leave my house now, and I will say nothing of these monstrous accusations of yours to anyone, provided you leave the city tonight. You would do well to take that offer, otherwise you will find yourself in prison. I have powerful friends in Bristol.'

I noticed the first flicker of doubt in Cicely's eyes as she glanced at her guardian, and pressed my advantage. 'I don't think you would hand me over to the sheriff or any of his officers, Master Herepath, because you know that I would be certain to repeat my accusations to them. They might grow suspicious that I was telling the truth and make their own inquiries. Mistress Ford, will you have the goodness to give me a hearing?'

There was a moment's silence before she answered firmly, 'Yes. Yes, I will. Edward, please don't be cross. It is only by listening to what Master Chapman has to say that you will be able to refute it.' She drew a stool close to the fire and sat down. Edward Herepath hesitated for a second, then resumed his own seat, defeated. Perhaps he hoped there was still a chance that I knew too little, or that he would be able to find specious answers to my allegations. Be that as it may, he made no further effort to prevent me speaking. Cicely gestured in my direction. 'Proceed, Master Chapman.'

For brevity's sake, I will set down my story as I told it

to Cicely Ford, but without detailing either her interruptions or her gradually diminishing exclamations of disbelief. Edward Herepath said nothing, but as my recital continued, he huddled deeper into his chair, his face growing ever more ashen, his whole demeanour giving weight and substance to my indictment. If Cicely Ford had doubts when I began, I think she had few by the time I had finished.

The paths of Edward Herepath and William Woodward crossed because they were both followers of John Wycliffe and believers in the Lollard heresy. They probably first encountered one another at one of the meetings in the cave in the great gorge, outside the city. Lollards foregathered – and for all I know still do – in such places, for lack of their own conventicles. Edward must have learned of William's discontentment with his lot, living with his widowed daughter, and dissatisfaction with his treatment by the Weavers' Guild. Five years earlier, therefore, he had offered William the job as his rent collector, when it had suddenly fallen vacant, together with the cottage in Bell Lane. And I guessed it to be Edward Herepath who had given William his English Bible, for the older man could never have afforded such a thing himself.

Although at the time it had been nothing more than a gesture of goodwill from one Lollard to another, the offer, and its acceptance, had later proved invaluable to Edward when the most pressing desire of his life became that of ridding himself of his brother. For barely a year after William Woodward was installed in his new job, John

Ford died, leaving his daughter and only child in Edward Herepath's care; and Cicely went to live in the house in Small Street. Edward fell instantly in love with his ward, but he was then still a married man, and in any case, Cicely had eyes and heart for no one but Robert.

A year later, Mary Herepath, Edward's wife, died, leaving him a free man. And from that moment on, Edward must have started planning how to get rid of his brother. It had to be in such a way that no blame could possibly attach to himself, but there was more to it than that. Mistress Walker had told me that nothing Robert did, however venal, seemed to lessen Cicely's affection for him. Therefore, to have him killed, as Edward Herepath had tried to have me killed, by hiring bravos from the Backs to do the deed, would only have made him a martyr in Cicely's eyes. No: it had to appear that Robert had committed a crime so heinous that even she would be unable to forgive him. And what could be more horrible than the murder of an old, defenceless man for gain?

But Robert Herepath could not be made to kill to order. He was a thief, a drunkard, a gambler, but not a murderer; so Edward had to make him seem one. He laid his plans carefully. The Lollard heresy was spreading, and about that time was reaching across the Severn. William, again according to his daughter, was a devoutly religious man, but with his own beliefs. I had no proof, but I was as certain as if I had overheard their conversation, that Edward Herepath had persuaded him it was his duty to go as an itinerant preacher into Wales, in spite of the attendant dangers. 'But when I eventually return,' William would have argued, 'how shall I explain my absence?' And so Edward had persuaded this simple man to lay a false trail, secure in the knowledge that he would never come back. 'Say you were captured by Irish slavers, but managed to escape. Do as I tell you and you will be believed.'

I remembered Margaret Walker telling me that William had been seen, late on the day of his disappearance, coming from the butcher's shop near All Hallows Church; and when I had watched her making black pudding on that morning some weeks since, I had suddenly realized that his purchase must have been sheep or ox blood, which, on Edward's instructions, he had daubed about his room. He had smeared some on his hat as well, which, under cover of darkness, he had dropped into the Frome. Also, when it was dark, he had left his cottage in Bell Lane and walked the little distance to the Small Street garden, where, in the outbuilding, he had changed into clothes which Edward had left for him before he himself set off for Gloucester earlier in the day. For it was essential that William should not be recognized when he left the city the following morning.

It was also necessary to Edward's plan that William should reach the vicinity of Gloucester by nightfall on the Friday, and therefore he could not travel on foot. He was given a key to the stable and instructed to take the bay, for had not the farrier told me that he and his master were the only two people who had the means to unlock the wicket gate? And so, dressed in Edward Herepath's clothes which, although the two men were much of a size, were just a little too small for him, and riding the bay, it was hardly surprising that Henry Dando had mistaken William Woodward for Edward Herepath in the dim light of that early Friday morning, as he turned from Magdalen Lane into Stony Hill and rode towards the windmill.

'Indeed,' I said, sparing a glance for the huddled figure in the armchair, 'it is less surprising than the fact that William was not "recognized" as you by the porter at the Frome Gate. But he was probably still half asleep, for I imagine that William began his journey as soon as it was light.'

'You imagine a great deal too much,' Edward Herepath sneered, but the sting had gone out of his words. I could see that Cicely's stillness frightened him: she was beginning to be convinced by my story. Nevertheless, he continued, 'And when William reached Gloucester, what then? If you have made inquiries at the New Inn, as I am sure you have, you will know that the only person to visit me there was Richard Shottery, from whom I bought the gelding.'

I nodded. 'But Master Woodward did not enter the city. On the Friday afternoon, having completed your purchase of the horse before dinner, you disappeared and only returned after dark. You told the landlord that you were the last man in at the West Gate before it closed.'

'So?'

'I think you met William Woodward, as you had already arranged, to escort him over the Severn and set him on his way through the forest into Wales. It would have been late in the day by that time, nearly dusk, and William would have been extremely weary, having ridden hard all day. His wits would be wool-gathering, thinking only of a meal and a bed. No doubt you pretended to be escorting him to some Lollard's cottage, where he would be provided with rest and refreshment for the night. Instead – ' I paused for a moment to give weight to my words – 'instead you persuaded him to dismount on some pretext or other, and while he sat on the ground to ease his aching limbs, you attacked him, belabouring him about the head with a bludgeon, or whatever else you had brought with you for the purpose, eventually leaving him for dead. You then rode back to Gloucester, wrapping yourself in your cloak to conceal any bloodstains there might have been on your clothing.'

'This is wicked talk, and I'll stand no more of it.' Edward Herepath made to rise, but Cicely forestalled him, getting up and placing herself between us, evidently afraid that he might once again assault me.

'Pray go on, Master Chapman,' she said quietly. 'What happened when my guardian returned to Bristol?' Her eyes were bright and huge, as though she were staring into an abyss at some unnamed horror.

'I think the rest you know. Master Herepath went first to the cottage in Bell Lane to see if William's apparent murder had been discovered and, more importantly, if the money were missing. Having reassured himself on both points, he hastened back to Small Street to search his brother's room and find the leather pouches where they had been hidden. The bloodstains on the bags and the breast of Robert's jerkin – where he had held them cradled in his left arm during his short journey home – were fortuitous, but added greatly to the weight of evidence against him. Even you, Mistress Ford, were convinced of Robert's guilt, and your reaction to so callous a crime was everything that Master Herepath had guessed it would be.

'All he had to do then was play the grieving brother who had at least reached the end of his tether; who could no longer stand between the youth he had raised from infancy and his manifold sins. Margaret Walker spoke of a kind of madness that seemed to grip the town. Alderman Weaver said dislike of Robert clouded his and everyone else's judgement. But I suggest it was partly because Edward Herepath let it be known, in as many quarters as possible, that he believed his brother guilty.'

'It is you who are mad!' Edward snarled. 'I was the only person who protested Robert's innocence.'

Cicely turned her head slowly to look at him. 'But you made it plain you didn't really believe what you said. Particularly when you gave your testimony at Robert's trial. That was what made your conviction of his guilt so obvious.' She lifted a hand to her forehead. 'You comforted me. We comforted one another for the loss of something we had both believed in; our faith that Robert, whatever his faults, was not truly wicked. We shared a great grief and it drew us close together.' She shuddered. 'It even crossed my mind that one day, perhaps, I might grow to love you as I had loved your brother.'

'Which was exactly what your guardian had hoped for,' I was quick to point out. 'And then, his plans all went awry when William Woodward made his sudden reappearance. You must have been terrified,' I went on, addressing Edward, 'when you heard of his return, when you realized that you had bungled your attempt at murder. But luck was with you. The injuries William had sustained had destroyed coherent memory. He could not even recall the cottage in Bell Lane, but went home to his daughter. All he could remember was that he must say he had been abducted by slavers and taken to Ireland; that for some good reason, he must not mention his time with the miners in the forest. And so you were safe, but not so safe that you could sleep soundly at nights.'

My voice grew sterner. 'You dreaded that William would regain his senses and reveal the truth. You refused to visit him with Mistress Ford, because you were frightened that the sight of you would bring back memories. Then your housekeeper told you that Mistress Ford was taking William broth, and you made another attempt to kill him. He complained of the broth tasting bitter, so his daughter and granddaughter threw it away. Margaret Walker attributes it to bad meat used by Mistress Hardacre in her cooking. But I suspect the soup contained juice of hemlock, which grows in your garden.' I took a deep breath and drew a bow at a venture. 'And for all I know, that's how your wife met her end, after you fell in love with Mistress Cicely.'

'You lie!' Edward Herepath croaked. 'You can prove none of it!'

'I can prove William Woodward was with the miners in the forest, and in what condition they found him. The landlord of the New Inn will testify to your movements on the Friday. I agree it might not be enough to condemn you in the eyes of the law, but it would suffice to breed suspicion amongst your fellow burgesses of this city.' I decided the moment had come to tell Master Herepath the one thing he did not already know. 'And all of it for nothing. For your hope of one day marrying Mistress Ford, in spite of everything, is a doomed one. She has set her heart on entering a religious order.'

Edward Herepath uttered a strange, tortured cry and turned his eyes on Cicely. He sprang to his feet and caught her in his arms. 'You cannot! You shall not! You are mine! We belong together. I have known it since the moment you came to live here. Until then, I foolishly thought of you as a child, but you had grown. I realized then that you were the one person in the world I really wanted.' His eyes glowed suddenly with a kind of madness, and I moved closer, ready to intervene. Cicely was staring at him in fascinated horror, as though at a stranger.

Edward went on: 'I rid myself of Mary, but you fell in love with Robert. That wastrel! I thought if I bided my time, you were bound to sicken of his wild and shiftless ways and turn to me for comfort. But nothing he could do changed your mind about him. In the end, I realized I should have to change it for you. He must be vilified in your eyes so that you would turn from him in horror. It was only what he deserved. It was done for your protection. And I so nearly succeeded. If William had died, as he should have done, there in the forest, no one would ever have known that Robert didn't murder him.' His arms tightened about her. 'You shan't deprive me of what I've killed for!'

Cicely said in a quiet voice, 'Let me go, Edward. I pity you with all my heart, for I think you must have sold your soul to the Devil. It was not Robert who was evil. He was just wild and selfish, but the real wickedness is in you. I have arranged to enter the House of the Magdalen Nuns as a postulant, and I shall do so now as soon as possible. I shall go there tonight, for my life in this accursed house is finished as from this hour. I shall not raise a hand against you, even though you have destroyed my life, but what Master Chapman does is up to him.'

I waited to see what would happen, ready if necessary to force him to release her, but the sight of her face, so filled with sorrow and loathing, acted on Edward Herepath as nothing else could. His love for her had grown into an obsession, until it drove out all other feelings, all notion of right and wrong; until he had been willing to kill, by whatever means, to win her for himself. The one person he could not harm was Cicely. His arms dropped to his sides. He sat down again and buried his face in his hands, his whole body racked with harsh, dry sobs. Without a backward glance, Cicely Ford turned and walked from the room.

After some seconds of indecision, I followed her. She had vanished into the upper regions of the house, and I waited until she came down again, still wearing her cloak and holding a large linen scrip which I imagined contained her night shift, brushes and combs. Then I escorted her to the House of the Magdalen Nuns before going in search of the sheriff and his officers. By the time they had returned from church, and I had told my story and convinced them sufficiently of its truth, it was dark and well past supper. I went back, accompanied by two sergeants, to Small Street. There we found a house in uproar: Mistress Hardacre and Dame Freda in hysterics, the men servants standing around, awe-struck, and Edward Herepath dead by his own hand. He had emptied the remains of his store of hemlock juice into the mazer of wine, sent in to him by the housekeeper with his supper.

There is little more to tell. He had written a full confession before he killed himself, a great shock to his fellow burgesses and townsmen, who had held him in such high esteem. But, like all these things, it was a nine days' wonder, and it was not long before some people began to claim they had always had their doubts about Edward Herepath, and could recall incidents which reflected badly on his character. As for myself, Lillis and I were married at the end of February in the weavers' church of St Catherine, in Temple Street; and my old acquaintance, Alderman Weaver, dignified the ceremony with his presence, standing with us in the porch and even deigning to enter the nave with us afterwards. My new mother-in-law was deeply impressed.

I should like to say that my marriage to Lillis was very happy for the sake of you, my dear daughter, my dear Elizabeth, should you ever read this. But you know me too well to expect anything but the truth. It was no happier, no more miserable a union than anyone else's, and we had so little time together, who can tell how it might have turned out? Suffice it to say that, when your mother died, giving birth to you on that bitterly cold November day, I felt bereft. Lillis was a part of my life, and the Lord, in His wisdom, had taken her away.